GOLD IN THE FIRE

MARGARET DALEY

Steeple
Hill®

Published by Steeple Hill Books™

STEEPLE HILL BOOKS

Steeple
Hill®

ISBN 0-373-87283-6

GOLD IN THE FIRE

Copyright © 2004 by Margaret Daley

www.SteepleHill.com

Printed in U.S.A.

What am I doing? Darcy thought. I have no business thinking about Joshua Markham in any terms other than a firefighter and an acquaintance.

She started to switch on the engine and leave before anyone knew they were at the firehouse. Too late. Joshua waved from the door and strode toward her and her son.

"See, he's expecting us," Sean said.

Darcy wanted to hide. She felt the heat suffuse her cheeks as the man walked to the truck, a smile of greeting on his face. The first thing she thought about was the dusty jeans she wore and the old, worn shirt. Why hadn't she changed before coming into town? And why did she care?

Joshua stopped on her side of the truck, his face framed in the window, only a few inches from her. She rolled down the window and forced a smile to her lips. "Is this a bad time to visit?"

Please let it be, she silently added, responding to his heart-melting grin. Her pulse accelerated.

* * *

Books by Margaret Daley

Love Inspired

The Power of Love #168
Family for Keeps #183
Sadie's Hero #191
The Courage To Dream #205
What the Heart Knows #236
A Family for Tory #245
*Gold in the Fire #273

*The Ladies of Sweetwater Lake

MARGARET DALEY

feels she has been blessed. She has been married for thirty-three years to her husband, Mike, whom she met in college. He is a terrific support and her best friend. They have one son, Shaun, who married his high school sweetheart in June 2002.

Margaret has been writing for many years and loves to tell a story. When she was a little girl, she would play with her dolls and make up stories about their lives. Now she writes these stories down. She especially enjoys weaving stories about families and how faith in God can sustain a person when things get tough. When she isn't writing, she is fortunate to be a teacher for students with special needs. Margaret has taught for over twenty years and loves working with her students. She has also been a Special Olympics coach and has participated in many sports with her students.

These have come so that your faith—
of greater worth than gold, which perishes
even though refined by fire—may be proved
genuine and may result in praise, glory and honor
when Jesus Christ is revealed.

—*1 Peter* 1:7

To Laura Marie Altom, a friend
who helped me find where I belonged as a writer.
Thank you.

To Paige Wheeler, my agent,
who has been a great support.
Thank you.

To Ann Leslie Tuttle and Diane Dietz,
my two editors at Love Inspired,
who have believed in me.
Thank you.

Chapter One

Darcy O'Brien's hands shook as she brushed her hair behind her ears. She stared down at her fingers, covered with soot, the black reminding her of the charred remains of the barn only yards away. The heat from the fire chased away the early-morning chill. Smoke curled upward from the darkened boards to disappear in the fog that had rolled in to encase her in a gray cocoon. But there was nothing protective and safe about her surroundings.

Eerie. Unearthly. Darcy shivered and hugged her arms to her.

"Ma'am?"

The sound of a deep, husky voice floated to her from the swirls of smoke and fog. Her eyes stung as she searched the yard. Emerging from the shroud of gray a man appeared, dressed in a black jacket with yellow strips and black pants. He removed his fire helmet and cradled it under his arm. Dark brown hair, damp from sweat, lay at odd angles. Black smudges highlighted the hard angles of his face and emphasized the blueness of his eyes. For just a moment Darcy thought of a warrior striding purposefully toward her.

"Yes, may I help you?" she asked, pushing away her fantasy.

"That man over there said you're the one in charge." The firefighter tossed his head in the direction of Jake, one of the grooms.

The idea that she was in charge weighed heavily on her shoulders, even though it was only for a few months. She straightened, ignoring the exhaustion that cleaved to every part of her. "Yes, I am."

The firefighter stuck his hand out. "I'm Joshua Markham. I conduct the arson investigations for the department."

"Arson?"

The strong feel of his handshake reassured her. For a few seconds she forgot the past couple of hours. Then she remembered pulling the frightened horses to safety, watching the barn go up in flames, the scent of burned wood heavy in the air. But mostly she remembered trying to persuade her father to return to the main house before he collapsed. That had been the hardest task of all.

"Yes, ma'am, it's definitely a possibility. This is the third barn fire in the past few weeks."

"Please call me Darcy. 'Ma'am' reminds me of my students."

He moved away from the pile of blackened rubble. Darcy followed. When she looked back toward the barn, all she saw was the swirls of fog. The stench of smoke clung to the air.

"When it's safe, I'll bring in my dog. I'll know more after I can take some samples and check the area out more thoroughly."

"Dog?" Her mind refused to grasp the implication of what he was saying.

"He'll be able to locate where the fire originated. We'll pinpoint what the accelerant was. If it matches the other fires, we'll know we have a serial arsonist on our hands."

"Serial arsonist? But why here?"

Joshua shrugged. "There are countless reasons why someone sets a fire. Most are for some kind of personal gain, but occasionally we find a person who just likes to set fires and watch them burn."

Darcy shuddered. Sweetwater was always such a quiet town, not like where she lived now. Even though there were nearly fifteen thousand people in Sweetwater, she still thought of it as a small, close-knit community.

"If it's arson, there'll be a thorough investigation."

"Of course."

"I'll be looking into all the reasons why someone would set a fire. That includes personal gain."

For a moment her mind went blank. Stunned, she couldn't think of a reply.

"Just thought I'd let you know."

"Why?"

"I know your father had a heart attack a few weeks

ago. Shamus Flanaghan is a respected member of our community. I don't think he had anything to do with this, but I still have to check out the possibility."

"And you want me to cushion the blow?"

The corner of his mouth quirked. "Yes, ma—Darcy. I would appreciate it."

"So in other words, you want me to help you with your investigation."

Joshua plowed his hand through his damp hair. "Well, not exactly. I just don't want to be responsible for causing your father further grief. But questions will have to be asked—and answered."

"Then you can ask me. As of last week, I'm acting as the manager of this farm until my father gets back on his feet." If she said it enough times, perhaps it would be true.

"I'll be back later with my camera and Arnold. I'll know more after I take a look around." He put his helmet on. "Good day."

Frustration churned in her stomach as she watched the firefighter walk away, the thick fog and smoke swallowing him until all she saw was a gray wall. Another shiver rippled down her spine. What in the world had she gotten herself into? A serial arsonist?

Normally this was her favorite time of day, when the sun was just peeking over the horizon, the sky lit with color, the birds chirping in the nearby trees. Even when it was foggy, there was a certain appeal to dawn, a mystery waiting to be uncovered. But now there was a real mystery. Who would want to set fires to barns filled with horses?

A pounding behind her eyes hammered at her temples. Her father raised jumpers and hunters. People from all over the country came to him. His reputation as a breeder had always been paramount to him—at times to the exclusion of even his family.

Darcy closed her eyes for a few seconds and tried to compose her shattered nerves. There was so much she had to do. She didn't know where to begin. Finally she decided she had to check on her father first, to make sure he was following his doctor's orders, before she could even take the time to assimilate this latest news.

She started up the road that led to the main house, white painted fences on either side of the asphalt. Somewhere out in those fields were some of their prize broodmares. But the fog that adhered to the ground obscured her view. She would need to make sure all the horses were accounted for—after she saw her father and reassured herself that he was all right.

She entered the house through the back door. Lizzy Johnson, the petite housekeeper, stood at the stove, shaking her head while she prepared French toast. A strand of gray hair fell forward on her forehead. With a heavy sigh, she brushed it back in place.

"What's wrong, Lizzy?"

"One thing. Shamus. He insists on eating a proper breakfast. He wanted eggs, bacon and toast. He's getting French toast. I figure that's better than a plate full of cholesterol-high eggs fried in bacon grease."

The frustration in Lizzy's voice matched her own feelings. Darcy knew how difficult her father could be.

He didn't like change, and the new diet his doctor wanted him on was definitely a change.

"I'll have a word with Dad. Is he in his room resting?"

Lizzy arched a brow. "Resting? No, he's dressed and ready to go back down to the barn."

"But he promised me—" Darcy swallowed the rest of her sentence. It was hopeless. Her father didn't know how to take it easy or to follow orders. Why had she thought she would be able to help her father recover when he had never slowed down for anything in the past, not even when her mother had died? He'd put in almost a full day of work the day of the funeral.

"Child, he's in the dining room drinking his coffee. Praise the Lord, decaf. But it was a battle to get him to drink that instead of regular coffee. I'm surprised you didn't hear it down at the barn." Lizzy flipped over the pieces of bread, her gaze clouding. "How bad is it?"

"Bad. The barn is completely gone. Thankfully no one was hurt, but we lost one mare in foal. The rest of the horses we managed to save. Now I have to handle finding places to stable seventeen mares until we can rebuild the barn." Darcy thought back to what Joshua Markham had said about a serial arsonist. What if the other barns were in danger?

"And a father who won't listen to his doctor's advice."

"Yes, that, too."

"Here, I suspect you could use some of this. Just keep it away from your father." Lizzy passed her a glass pot full of a dark brown brew. "This has lots of caffeine."

"Thanks. I can always count on you, Lizzy," Darcy murmured as she made her way into the dining room.

Pausing halfway down the long, cherry-wood table that seated twelve, she put the pot on a thick place mat. Then, instead of sitting, she gripped the back of a brocade-covered chair, leaning into it for support.

Her father glanced up from reading the newspaper. "I thought you were Lizzy with the breakfast she insists I eat. What's taking her so long? Never mind—I'm sure she's not hurrying because she doesn't think I should go down to the barn."

"You shouldn't, Dad. I can take care of everything. Did you rest at all?"

He frowned. "Rest when one of my barns is burning? What do you think?"

"When did you come back to the house?"

He looked away, busying himself with taking several sips of his coffee.

"Dad?"

"Thirty minutes ago." His sharp eyes returned to her face. "Did you really think I would go back to the house and sleep? I thought you knew me better than that."

Darcy took in the tired lines etched into his weathered face, an ashen cast to it. She noticed the slump to his shoulders and the slight trembling as he brought the cup to his lips. He was barely holding himself together, and she didn't know how to make him stop and rest before he— She wouldn't think about what could happen to him if he didn't do what the doctor said. Their relationship might not be a strong one, but he was her father and she cared.

"Dad, there isn't anything you can do now. I can take care of stabling the mares and seeing to the mess. That's why I came home to help you."

"When I agreed to you coming home to help, it wasn't for something like this. I could have lost a third of my breeding stock last night."

Her grip on the chair tightened until pain shot up her arms. "I'm capable of handling it."

"This is *my* life." He thumped his chest. "I need to see to it."

Darcy pulled out the chair and sat before she collapsed. The long night was finally catching up with her, and she felt the lack of sleep in every fiber of her being.

"If you don't take care of yourself and follow the doctor's orders, there will be no life to see to."

"You don't mince words."

"You've always taught me to tell it like it is. You've been home from the hospital only a few days. You aren't supposed to deal with anything stressful, especially something like what happened last night."

He leaned forward, clasping the edge of the table. "Don't you understand, not knowing is more stressful than seeing to my job."

"I came up here to check on you, then I intend to return to make sure everything is taken care of. I'll report back to you as soon as I deal with stabling the mares. I'll keep you informed as if you're right there." The tightness in her throat threatened to cut off her words. She swallowed several times and continued. "Please let me do this for you." *Please, for once in your life, need me.*

For several moments he stared at her. Then suddenly he slumped back in the chair and dropped his head. "You win. *This* time. But I don't intend to stay in my room for long. Just as soon as I feel a little better, I'll be down at the barn."

The weak thread to his words, the fact that he'd backed down, underscored how sick her father really was. He would never admit more than he had, but she knew he was definitely feeling the effects of being up most of the night.

"Then you'll go rest and wait for me to come see you?"

He nodded.

Darcy poured herself some coffee, her hands trembling as much as her father's had. She didn't particularly like the bitter taste, but she needed a lot of caffeine to keep herself going. She decided to tell her father later about what Joshua Markham had said concerning the fire probably being the work of an arsonist. Until Joshua confirmed it, she didn't want to upset her father any more than he already was. But if there was someone going around setting fire to barns, the next few months would be more difficult than she had anticipated. Somehow she had to protect her father, even though he would fight her every inch of the way. Maybe then she would live up to what he expected.

* * *

From the paddock Darcy saw Joshua with a big black dog exploring the pile of burned rubble that had once been the broodmare barn. This afternoon was so different from earlier, when smoke had lingered in the air and the sun had been obscured. Now the sun's rays touched her face and warmed her skin. The sweet smell of freshly mowed grass peppered the air, almost wiping away the memory of the fire, the smell of charred wood—until she looked at the destruction the flames had caused.

With a sigh, she made her way toward Joshua, who ducked under the yellow tape that cordoned off the area. He strode toward his pickup with his dog on a leash and holding two metal cans.

"Did you find anything?" she asked, catching herself staring at the man, dressed in his navy-blue firefighter's uniform, his badge glittering in the sunlight. She forced herself to look down at the dog at his side before he found her staring at him.

He stored the metal cans alongside some others in the back of his truck, then secured a tarpaulin over them. "Not sure until the lab report comes back, but Arnold was very interested in several spots. I took some samples."

"He's a beauty." She rubbed the black Labrador retriever behind his ears. "How long have you had him?"

"Three years. He's garnishing quite a reputation in the state."

"Reputation?"

"He's ninety- to ninety-five-percent accurate when pinpointing the accelerant in a fire. Much better than the machine we used to have." Joshua opened the cab door and indicated to the dog to jump inside. "So when there's a questionable fire, Arnold and I get called out."

"Does that keep you busy?"

"Sometimes."

Arnold poked his head out the open window and prodded Darcy with his nose. She laughed and scratched him behind his ears some more.

"He likes you."

"I love animals."

The blue gleam in his eyes dimmed. "I'm sorry about the horse you lost in the fire."

"She was in foal. My son took it quite hard."

"Son? Was that the young man down here when I came?"

"Probably. Red hair, freckles, eight?"

"Yep. He had a few questions to ask me."

"Just a few?"

"Well, more like twenty." Joshua leaned against the cab of the truck, folding his arms across his chest.

"You got off easy. His curiosity will get him into trouble one day. I'm surprised he isn't still here."

"Said something about helping with a foal."

Darcy peered toward the second broodmare barn a paddock away. "Yes, we had one born last night. That's where I was when the fire broke out."

"It seems last night was an eventful night for you."

"And one I don't want to repeat anytime soon."

"I need to talk with your father. When would be a good time?"

"He's resting right now. I'd rather not disturb him. He didn't get any sleep last night."

"Did you?"

The probe of Joshua's gaze caused her to blush. She must look a sight—with circles under her eyes and some soot from the fire probably still on her face. She hadn't even taken the time to clean up properly. She raised her hand to wipe at her cheeks as if that would erase any evidence of the night before.

"No, not for thirty-six hours. I tried to take a nap a few hours ago, but when I closed my eyes, all I saw were flames."

"That sounds like one of my dreams. One of the hazards of being a firefighter, I guess." He pushed away from the truck. "I need to ask you some questions too. I've already interviewed the others who were here last night."

A shiver shimmered down her length when she thought back to the night before. "I'm not sure I can be of much help. All I was thinking about was getting the horses to safety." The memory of the one mare she hadn't been able to save pierced through her armor. The horse's cries would haunt her for a long time.

"I need to drop these samples off, then I'll take Arnold home. After that, I'll be back to talk to you and your father." Joshua started past her, stopped and twisted back around. "I wish we had met under better circumstances."

"So do I."

"I know this can't be easy coming home to all this."

That was definitely an understatement, she thought. But she never shared her worries with others. She'd learned a long time ago to keep her concerns to herself. She was about to make a light comment when her son appeared in the yard, yelling to get their attention. He raced toward them, skidding to a halt next to her.

Sean smiled up at Joshua. "Oh, good. You haven't left yet. Mom, did you meet Arnold? Isn't he neat? He has the best nose in the state. When something smells wrong, he'll sit."

Darcy laughed. "This chatterbox is my son, Sean O'Brien, just in case he forgot to tell you his name before."

"How's the foal?" Joshua asked, coiling the dog leash in his hand.

"She's a filly. She's all legs."

"Sorta like you, sweetie." Darcy hugged Sean to her, rubbing his head. "He's going through another one of his growth spurts."

"Aw, Mom." He squirmed from her embrace, a red tint to his cheeks that made his freckles stand out. "Do you wanna see the filly? You can pet her."

"I wish I could, but I have to finish my job first. Can I take a rain check on that offer?" Joshua tossed the leash into the truck.

"Sure. Just let me know. I know Grandpa won't mind."

"Speaking of Grandpa, did you finish mucking out those stalls you promised him you would do each day?"

Sean dropped his head, his chin on his chest.

"Just as I suspected, young man. You know he'll ask you about that when he gets up from his nap."

"I've got one done." Sean began to run toward the broodmare barn, came to a stop and glanced back at Joshua. "Don't forget about the filly."

"I won't. I'll be back out here later. Maybe you can show me then."

Beaming, Sean shouted, "Yes," and continued toward the far barn.

"Thank you."

Joshua's eyebrows rose. "For what?"

"For taking some time out of your busy schedule to see the filly." *For not rejecting my son's interest,* she added silently, thinking about all the times her husband had dismissed Sean's enthusiasm, never having any time for him.

"I'm not that busy that I can't take a little time to see an animal."

The smile that accompanied his words melted defenses that she had erected over the years. "I must warn you, if you allow him Sean will whittle his way into your life."

"I know several nice boys his age that go to my church. I would be glad to introduce him to them."

"I'm sure he'd like that. He's always in the thick of things back home."

"I understand that your father used to go to my church. From what I hear he was quite active at one time. His attendance has been spotty these past few years."

"Don't you mean nonexistent?"

Joshua kneaded the back of his neck. "Well, now that you put it that way, yes. He hasn't been in quite some time."

"More than likely thirteen or fourteen years."

"Maybe this Sunday you can get your father to attend again."

"No one can get him to do anything he doesn't want to."

"I understand." He grinned. "I need to go. I'll be back later." Joshua walked around the front of his truck and got in.

As the red pickup drove away, Darcy turned toward the burned barn. Yellow tape marked off the area, preserving the charred structure for Joshua's investigation. Scanning the pile of rubble, she couldn't imagine any evidence being left. The fire had consumed most of the barn with nothing untouched by its flames. They would have to raze the building and start over—much as she had after Clay's death.

"That must be Joshua Markham." Darcy rose from the couch when she heard the sound of an approaching vehicle.

Sean hopped up. "I'll get it."

Her father watched him race from the room. "Where does he get all that energy? I could use some."

"He's excited that Joshua's visiting."

"I expected he would have questions, especially since the Andersons' and Bakers' barns burned."

"Why didn't you tell me two other barns have burned down in the past month?"

"Didn't think it pertained to us." Beneath his usual tanned features, his skin had a sickly pallor. "Guess I was wrong. Don't see why anyone would want to go around killing horses."

Darcy heard her son's chattering as he escorted Joshua toward the den. "Shh, Dad. I don't want to frighten Sean any more than he already is. He took the mare's death hard."

"Then he shouldn't be here for the interview," her father murmured in a gruff voice, shifting in his chair as both Joshua and Sean entered the room.

"Good afternoon, Mr. Flanaghan. I hope you're feeling better."

"Shamus, please. Mr. Flanaghan makes me sound so old, and I refuse to acknowledge I'm a day over thirty." Her father waved Joshua to the couch next to Darcy. "Sean, weren't you going to help Ken with the tack?"

"Yes, but—"

"No buts, young man. Scoot."

"I want to show Joshua the new filly."

"I'll bring Joshua down to the barn before he leaves so you can show him the foal," Darcy said, aware of the man sitting only a few inches from her. The couch suddenly seemed small with Joshua's large frame next to her.

Sean stuck out his lower lip and trudged toward the door, dragging his feet. "Okay, but don't forget."

"I won't let her," Joshua said as her son disappeared

into the hallway. Joshua removed a small pad of paper from his pocket along with a pen. "I have a few questions—"

Shamus held up his hand, then placed his forefinger over his lips. "Wait a sec," he whispered. After a few seconds they heard the sound of the front door closing, and he continued. "Little boys have big ears, and Darcy doesn't want to discuss the fire in front of Sean. If you ask me, she's overprotecting him, but I'll respect her wishes."

"Dad!" A blush singed her cheeks. "I just don't think discussions about fires and horses dying is what he needs to hear."

"You have a smart boy there, Darcy. He knows exactly what happened last night."

She angled toward Joshua. "What do you want to know?" This was neither the time nor the place to get into an argument with her father concerning her methods of raising Sean. In the short time she'd been home, he'd made it plain he thought she was overprotective. There wasn't much she could say to change her father's mind.

Joshua's gaze riveted to hers, a serious expression in his eyes. "Where were you when the fire broke out?"

Chapter Two

Joshua's question brought Darcy firmly back to the business at hand—the fire. "As I said earlier, I was in the other broodmare barn helping to deliver a foal." She knew the query was necessary, but it still bothered her.

Joshua wrote something on his pad, then asked her father, "And you, sir?"

Shamus's mouth twisted into a frown as he peered away. "I was working in the office on the books."

"Dad! You were supposed to be asleep."

"Well, I wasn't. I was just checking to make sure all the orders were made."

"I did those yesterday morning, Dad—" Darcy snapped her mouth closed, suddenly remembering they had an audience.

Silence hung in the air until her father cleared his throat and said, "I didn't know anything was happening at the barn until the alarm sounded. By the time I arrived, it was engulfed in flames."

Joshua shifted toward Darcy. "What did the fire look like when you arrived?"

"Not much better. Smoke was everywhere and flames were beginning to shoot out the east side."

"And you went into the barn to get the horses out?"

"Yes. Jake was already bringing a few out. I managed to open the stall doors so the mares would at least have a chance to run to safety." The sounds of the frightened horses filled her mind all over again. Memories of the smoke-laden barn, the scent of fire everywhere, made her hug her arms to warm her chilled body.

"Did you see anything unusual or anyone who shouldn't have been there?"

Darcy shook her head, having gone over the scene many times in the past few hours, trying to come up with something that would explain the fire.

"Are you having any financial problems?"

Darcy was about to answer when her father cut in with a chuckle and said, "I wondered when you would ask me that. No, Shamrock Stables is doing fine. You may look at my books anytime. I don't need insurance money to pay my bills."

Surprised by her father's calm answer, Darcy pressed her lips together to keep from expressing her astonishment.

"Can you think of anyone, sir, who might have a grudge against you and the farm?"

"I try to do right by people, but I've made a few enemies in my lifetime." Her father drummed his fingers on the arm of the leather-padded chair, a distant look in his gray eyes. "Have Ray Anderson or John Baker thought of anyone?"

"A few disgruntled employees, but no one who has worked for both of them. Do any of your employees smoke?"

"Not around my barns. I have strict rules about that. I had to fire a groom back about six months ago because he kept forgetting it. Caught him smoking while he was mucking out a stall. Sent him packing that very minute."

"Who was that, sir?"

"Angus Feehan."

Joshua jotted down the name.

"Was it started with a cigarette?" Darcy asked, thinking back to how fast the fire had developed and spread. It had only been seven, maybe eight minutes before she'd had to escape the barn or be trapped inside.

"I found a butt near where I think the fire started, but I don't think it was the sole cause." Joshua rose, sliding the notepad into his pants pocket. "That's all for the time being."

Shamus started to stand, seemed to decide against it and remained seated, a pinch to his mouth indicating exhaustion. "I'd like to be kept informed of your investigation. I want to know if there's a connection to the other two fires."

"I'll let you know when I get the reports back from the lab. But from what I've seen so far, it looks like there is a connection."

Darcy came to her feet. "Let me show you the foal."

"I can find my way to the barn if you're busy."

"That's okay. I need to check on the mares we stabled in that barn. Make sure they're settled into their new home."

Out on the front veranda Darcy paused and took a deep breath. There was still a hint of burned wood in the air, but mostly the scent of grass, flowers and earth laced the breeze. She looked toward the horizon and noticed the sun beginning its descent. A few streaks of orange and pink threaded through the blue sky like pieces of ribbon carelessly tossed about.

"It's getting close to dinnertime, Mr. Markham. Would you like to stay and eat with us?"

"Please, call me Joshua, and yes, I would like that. I don't particularly care for my own cooking."

"Neither do I." Chuckling, Darcy blushed. "I mean *my* cooking, not yours."

"You wouldn't care for mine, either."

"I think we have established we're both lousy cooks." Darcy led the way toward the broodmare barn set off to the left and farthest from the house. "I promised myself when I came this summer to have Lizzy teach me some of her dishes. Of course, now I'm wondering when I'll find the time, what with the fire and all."

"Maybe I should throw myself on Lizzy's mercy, too."

"You know Lizzy?"

"Oh, yes. She's a mainstay at Sweetwater Community Church."

"That's right. I'd forgotten that's where my mother found her and asked her to be our housekeeper."

"How long has she been working for your family?" Joshua opened a gate and stepped to the side to allow Darcy to go first into a pasture that shortened the trip to the farthest barn.

"Fourteen years. Mom died not too long after Lizzy came to work for us." One of the mares in the paddock trotted over to Darcy and nudged her. She laughed and dug into the pocket of her black jeans for a few sugar cubes, holding her palm out flat. "Bluebell won't let me leave without getting some sweets from me. She's spoiled rotten." She ran her hand over the horse's dark brown flank. "She knows she's my favorite and uses that to her advantage."

Joshua walked around the mare, making sure the horse knew where he was at all times. "She's a beauty. When is she due?"

"Not for another month. I can't wait. She always has a beautiful foal." Darcy patted Bluebell on the rump before continuing toward the far end of the field where the broodmare barn was located.

"I wish I had more time to ride."

"You're in horse country. How can you not ride?" Again Joshua opened the gate and waited for Darcy to go first. "I know. Life gets in the way."

When Darcy entered the barn, the scents of hay and horses permeated the air. They made her feel as though she had come home. For the past ten years, since her marriage to Clay, she had spent all of her time other places—many other places—while her husband pursued his fighter-pilot career in the Navy. With his death the year before, everything had changed…and yet it hadn't. She wasn't sure what she should do with her life.

"Mom! Joshua! Come have a look. She's feeding." At the other end of the barn Sean danced in front of a stall with the biggest grin on his face. As they neared, he darted inside.

"I can see your son loves the farm," Joshua said with a laugh.

"Definitely." Darcy went into the stall with Joshua following, pushing away the guilty feeling she suddenly experienced. But it still niggled. She hadn't wanted to come home; she hadn't brought her son to see his grandfather until now.

"See. Isn't she neat?" Sean pointed to the foal nursing. "She lets me touch her. She almost fell once but she didn't."

Darcy inspected the foal who was all legs and still wobbly. The chestnut-colored coat reminded Darcy of the foal's mother. She hoped she was as good a jumper as her mother. Despite the fire, seeing the filly caused Darcy's hopes to rise. Life continued even amid problems.

"Grandpa said I could name her." Sean continued to stroke the foal.

"Have you come up with one yet?" Darcy asked, remembering the first time her father had let her name a horse—a lifetime ago. So much had happened to her in the last twenty-four years, and yet her relationship with her father was the same—strained, at best.

"I was thinking of Big Red, but that sounds like a boy. What do you think, Joshua?"

Joshua cocked his head and thought for a moment. "You're probably right. The correct name will come to you. After spending some time with her, I'm sure you'll come up with something that fits. Naming something is important."

Sean straightened, his shoulders thrown back, his big grin spreading even more. "I think so. I can't just give her any ol' name. Something real special." He peered around Joshua. "Where's Arnold? I was hoping to see him again."

"He's at home. He worked hard today so I gave him a treat and he's resting up. I'll bring him back some other time."

"I never met a fire dog before."

"There aren't a lot of them around."

"How did you come up with the name Arnold?"

"My first fire captain was named Arnold. He showed me the ropes. I wanted to honor him so I named Arnold after him."

Sean placed his forefinger on his chin. "Hmm. That's a thought."

"Well, young man, right now you need to get up to the house and wash up before dinner. You know how Lizzy is about clean hands."

"But, Mom, you and Joshua just got here."

"Joshua's coming to dinner, so you can talk to him at the table. That is, if you pass Lizzy's inspection."

"I will." He raced from the stall.

Joshua chuckled. "I don't think I've ever been used as a bribe to get someone to wash up."

"As a parent you learn to use any trick you can."

"I'm flattered."

"My son was quite taken with you and Arnold."

His smile reached deep into his blue eyes. "Maybe I can bring Arnold out here one day."

"You'll make my son's day." Darcy left the stall, and after closing its door, led the way into the barn to check each of the newly arrived mares to make sure they were settled. Joshua's quiet study of her heightened her awareness of him.

Outside, a line of oaks and maples hid the sun, dusk beginning to settle over the yard. "What made you become an arson investigator?" she asked, relishing the breeze caressing her face, cooling her cheeks.

"I decided it was the best of both worlds."

"What worlds?"

"When I was growing up, I would fluctuate between wanting to be a firefighter and a police officer. I fight fires, but I also investigate any that are suspicious in nature."

"Do you have many in Sweetwater?" Darcy thought of her hometown and the people she knew and couldn't imagine too many arsonists in the bunch.

"No, not usually, but with Arnold I cover more than just this area of Kentucky."

"But now there's a chance you have a serial arsonist in Sweetwater?"

Joshua paused at the gate to the paddock. Rolling his

shoulders, he rubbed the back of his neck, apparently trying to massage a stiffness. "It's looking like that. If these fires continue, someone is going to die. I have to stop the person before that."

"You think it's one person?"

"Most likely. That's how arsonists work usually."

Darcy again stopped and greeted Bluebell before continuing across the pasture toward the main house. "Do you usually catch an arsonist?"

"Arson cases are difficult to prosecute."

She quaked at the thought that the person responsible for setting three barn fires so far would go unpunished. A mare died last night, but that could have been a person trapped in the barn. *She* could have been trapped in the barn if Jake hadn't insisted she get out before she had a chance to save the last mare. That she wasn't able to help the horse plagued her, making it doubly important that they discover who set the fire. "Then your job is quite a challenge," she murmured, hoping this case was an exception.

"Especially when we have random fires with no apparent reason. It's one thing when someone burns down a building to collect the insurance money or for some other financial reason. Usually we can catch that person. But with no connection between the fires, it's hard to know what's motivating the arsonist."

"Didn't you say some people burn buildings just to watch them burn?"

"Yes, but I don't think that's what's happening here."

Darcy mounted the steps to the veranda. "Why?"

Joshua frowned, looking back toward the place where the burned rumble of the barn lay in a large mound. "Call it a hunch. Just a feeling I can't shake. Something's driving this person—something to do with farms, barns, horses."

"That doesn't narrow down too many people in and around Sweetwater, with this being in the middle of the Bluegrass area of Kentucky."

"I know. I have my work cut out for me." Joshua held the front door open for Darcy. "But from what I understand, running a farm isn't an easy task. I'd say you have your work cut out for you, too."

"It has been a while since I worked with the horses. Until I got married, I was learning the ropes from my father while attending college." *And not doing quite the job he wanted,* Darcy thought, remembering her father's frowns and remarks when she didn't do something his way.

"Sean told me his dad died last year."

"What *hasn't* my son told you?" Darcy stopped in the middle of the entry hall and faced Joshua, thinking of her son's enthusiasm and lack of inhibition. As the saying goes, he'd never met a stranger—which thankfully had helped him make friends. They had moved a lot over the years.

"We talked this afternoon for twenty minutes non-stop."

Darcy laughed. "Nonstop on whose part, yours or his?"

"Mostly his."

"That's what I thought. He doesn't know how to keep a secret. Whenever he gets me a present, I have to open it right then and there, because he can't wait. So this past Christmas I got his picture frame he made me on December fourth, the day he finished it."

"He said something about his dad dying in a plane crash."

"Clay was a fighter pilot for the Navy. During a routine exercise he had problems with his plane and crashed. Knowing the risks he had to take in his job, I thought I was prepared. I wasn't—" A tightness in her throat prevented her from saying anything else. In fact, she wasn't even sure why she had told Joshua that. But for some reason the man was easy to talk to, and for a year she had kept a lot bottled up inside her. For most of her life she'd held her emotions close to her heart.

"I'm sorry. Death of a loved one is always difficult. I've lost both my parents over the past eight years. They were the only family I had."

A profound sadness and empathy edged each of his words and drew Darcy to him. "You didn't grow up here, did you?" Darcy felt that she would have remembered someone like him, even though she suspected a few years separated them in age.

"No. Louisville. I moved here nine years ago. I didn't want to live in a large town, but I still wanted to be close if my parents needed me."

Darcy could tell from the tone in his voice that there was more to that story. Indeed there was more to Joshua Markham than merely being a firefighter. But she was only going to be here for a few months. With her heart still scarred from her marriage to Clay, there was no way she would open herself up to any more pain, to another man.

"Mom. Joshua." Sean came running into the entry hall and slid to a stop a few feet from Darcy. "Dinner is ready. Lizzy made my favorite."

"Pizza?" Darcy breathed a sigh of relief. Suddenly the atmosphere between her and Joshua had shifted and become charged with possibilities that she wouldn't pursue.

"Naw. Spaghetti. It's my favorite now."

Darcy clasped her son's shoulder and ruffled his hair. "You have a new favorite every week. I can't keep up with them anymore."

Sean blushed and leaned closer to Joshua, cupping his mouth as though he were imparting a deep, dark secret. "Anything Lizzy makes is my favorite. She's a great cook. Wait 'til you taste her spaghetti. Mom, you should get Lizzy to show you how."

"I doubt I could match her in that department."

"Sure, Mom. You can do anything. Jake told me about the yearlings you used to break."

"A long time ago. At the ripe old age of thirty-one I'm wiser now." She placed a hand on the small of her back. "Just thinking about those days I can feel the aches and pains. Every once in a while there was one who didn't like the feel of a bit and rein or the touch of a saddle and loved to show me how much."

Sean's eyes grew round. "Did you ever break anything?"

"Only my pride from time to time."

"Maybe I can learn how?"

"Not 'til you're much older." Then in a whisper to Joshua she added, "And gone from my home."

"Mom, I heard that."

"Come on. Let's go in to eat."

When Sean raced ahead, she reached out and touched Joshua's arm to stop his forward movement. The instant her fingers grazed him she pulled her hand away.

"Will you do me a favor, Joshua?"

"What?"

"Let's not talk about the fire at dinner tonight. Dad may bring it up, but I'd rather not get him too upset."

"Sure. I don't have anything else to share about the fire until I get the lab tests back."

"Knowing my father, he'll try to pump you for information about your investigation. The doctor said he needed to reduce his stress level, which I'm not sure is possible, especially now with the fire. But I'm going to do everything I can to make his life less stressful." Will that satisfy her father...finally? she wondered.

"Good luck. I've found if the person doesn't want change, it's nearly impossible to force one on them."

"I know, especially someone as stubborn as my father. But that's why I'm here this summer."

"So in August you'll be returning home. Sean said you lived in Panama City, Florida."

"Yes, I'm a high school librarian, so luckily I could take the summer off to help Dad. This trip will be good for Sean." She wasn't so sure about herself, especially after the rocky start she and her dad had had.

"You haven't come home much?"

Darcy thought of the estranged relationship between her and her father. "No, since Clay was in the Navy we were always moving, getting settled in at a new place." She started forward, not wanting to go into the past. Going backward wouldn't change what had happened and she was tired of trying to justify why it had taken a crisis to bring her home.

After they washed their hands, Darcy stepped into the dining room as Lizzy finished putting the last serving bowl on the table. The older woman turned to leave. "Why don't you stay and join us for dinner?" Darcy asked.

Lizzy looked startled. Shaking her head she began backing toward the door. "I've got too much to do in the kitchen."

"Lizzy, you're part of the family and you have to eat." Darcy inhaled the aroma of meat sauce, seasoned with oregano, garlic and onion, flavoring the air. "It smells wonderful." She sensed Joshua's presence behind her, and a tingling awareness shivered down her spine.

Lizzy glanced toward Shamus, who was already dishing up his spaghetti. "I don't—"

"Come on, Lizzy. Joshua's joining us." Sean took the bowl from his grandfather and spooned a big helping onto his plate.

The older woman sighed. "I guess, just this once."

"I've been trying to get her to join me for dinner for years," Shamus grumbled, a frown creasing his brow. "Always said she was too busy. We must have the cleanest kitchen in the state."

"You're welcome to eat in the kitchen anytime you want." Bristling, Lizzy sat next to Sean, leaving the other side of the table for Darcy and Joshua.

Shamus motioned toward the two empty chairs. "Sit, you two. I'm hungry and this is getting cold."

"I like cold spaghetti, Grandpa."

"You like anything that doesn't move." Shamus picked up the bowl of salad but didn't put any on his plate. He passed it to Sean with a smug look thrown toward Lizzy.

The older woman pinched her lips together and focused on filling her plate with the main course. She held her petite frame rigid in the chair, her movements jerky.

At the door Darcy twisted partway around to look at Joshua. "You can always reconsider eating with us. I forget how—" She couldn't come up with an acceptable way to describe the stressful, tension-laden meals she had spent with her father over the years. He was so set in his ways that he wouldn't even eat in the kitchen when it was just him. Darcy was sure that for the past thirty-five years her father had eaten in the dining room and that was the way it would remain.

"Your father reminds me of my own."

"He does?"

"Gruff on the outside, but mush on the inside."

"Mush?" What was Joshua seeing that she had missed? Darcy wondered.

"Look at him with your son. He's listening to every word he's saying."

Darcy glanced over her shoulder at her father. His gaze was glued to Sean, who was regaling him with details of the new foal's first day. Seeing the attention her son was getting pierced defenses she'd built up over the years when trying to deal with her father.

Darcy moved into the room, continuing to feel Joshua's presence close behind her. Had her relationship with her husband colored hers with her father? Even when Clay had been home, he had rarely shown any interest in Sean. Her son was starved for male attention, and that had provoked over the years memories of her own childhood: trying to please her father and never quite succeeding.

After she slipped into the chair across from Lizzy, she filled her plate with the delicious-smelling spaghetti and meat sauce, then gave the bowls to Joshua, who took the last bit. Her father and Sean had already started eating. Lizzy cleared her throat.

Shamus looked up, confusion darkening his expression. "What?"

"I would like to say a blessing," Lizzy said in a prim and proper voice.

Eyebrows slashing downward, Shamus released his fork to clang onto his plate. "Fine."

Lizzy and Joshua bowed their heads. Watching Joshua, Sean immediately followed suit. Darcy clasped her hands together, realizing they were quivering, and stared down at her plate, feeling her father's gaze drill into her.

"Dear Heavenly Father, bless this food we are about to partake of and watch out for each one at this table. Give us the strength to seek Your guidance and the power to know when we need Your help. Amen."

Darcy lifted her head. Her father snatched up his fork, grumbling something under his breath. When her mother died, he'd stopped going to church, telling Darcy that he was just too busy. She had gone with Lizzy until she had left home, but she had always been aware of her father's disapproval.

"Grandpa, Joshua's bringing Arnold here for me to play with. I wish I had a dog."

"We'll just see what we can do about that." Darcy was about to say something when her father continued. "Every boy should have a dog."

"Dad didn't like animals. And when we lived over- seas, it was hard to have one," Sean said.

"Arnold recently became a father. The puppies are five weeks old," Joshua said as he poured ranch dress- ing onto his salad.

Sean's eyes grew big. "They are? Can I have one?"

"A friend of mine owns them. I can check—" Joshua swung his gaze to Darcy "—if that's okay with your mom."

The full force of his attention was directed at Darcy, causing heat to steal into her cheeks. The urge to shift nervously in her chair inundated her. "I love dogs. That sounds great." She crossed her legs, then uncrossed them. "But, Sean, you'll have to learn to take care of your puppy. It's a big responsibility."

Her son puffed out his chest. "I'm eight, Mom. I'm big enough."

"And we need to see about getting him a horse while he's here this summer." Shamus pinned Darcy with his eyes. "You had one at the age of five."

Memories assailed Darcy. She balled the napkin in her lap, her nails digging into the soft cotton material.

"My very own horse?" Sean exclaimed.

"For as long as you're here and whenever you come to visit again. It would be nice if you visited every summer."

Again Darcy felt her father's intimidating glare. She returned it with an unwavering look, though memories of never quite living up to what her father expected continued to flit through her mind, scene after disappointing scene.

"Can I, Mom?" Sean bounced up and down in his chair.

"We'll see, hon."

"Yes!" Her son pumped his fist into the air. "A dog *and* a horse."

"Your mother's right about taking care of your animals. Around my farm that is a must." Shamus broke off a piece of French bread and started to reach for the butter.

"That isn't on your diet," Lizzy said, snatching away the butter dish before his fingers touched it.

"Nothing good is on my diet," Shamus grumbled, his mouth puckered in a frown.

Before her father started in on what he couldn't eat anymore, Darcy released the tight grip on her napkin and asked, "Joshua, what made you decide to work with a dog?"

"I've been known to take in strays. My captain knew I loved animals, especially dogs, so when this opportunity came up, he encouraged me to do it. Arnold and I went through some extensive training, but it's been worth it."

"Heard you helped solve the Wright case a few months back." With narrowed eyes, Shamus stared at the butter dish sitting next to Lizzy's plate and just out of his reach.

"Wright case? What happened?" Darcy watched the silent exchange between her father and Lizzy—a battle of gazes. In the end her father turned his attention to Joshua. Darcy's mouth almost fell open.

"It was a warehouse fire in Lexington that spread to some other buildings. It was arson. We were lucky and apprehended the man responsible."

"Who?"

"An employee who had been fired and was angry at the owner."

"I came up with another name of someone you could check out," Shamus said, lifting his water glass to take a big sip. "I'd forgotten I had to let Mike Reynolds go a couple of months ago."

"He was your assistant farm manager, wasn't he?" Joshua asked, peering at Darcy.

Did he notice the stiff set to her shoulders and the tight grip she had on her glass? she wondered.

"Yeah. I didn't like his methods."

"He's working at the Colemans' farm now."

"That's what I heard."

"Dad, I think—"

Shamus swung his sharp gaze toward his daughter, a challenge in his eyes.

Darcy stiffened even more. "I don't think we need to discuss this at the dining room table." She glanced toward her son.

"Aw, Mom, I know about the fire."

"You know, Lizzy, I have to agree with Darcy. You're a terrific cook." Joshua took another bite of his spaghetti. He wished he could ease the heavy tension in the room.

The vulnerability he glimpsed in Darcy's eyes melted through his defenses. He found himself wanting to help her through the pain he knew she was experiencing. Her smile touched his heart, urging him to comfort. After Carol's betrayal he hadn't thought that possible, and was surprised by the feeling.

Lizzy blushed a nice shade of red, her eyes twinkling. "You always do know just the right thing to say, Joshua Markham."

Shamus snorted but continued eating.

Sean added, "He's right. I love your spaghetti."

Darcy slid a glance toward Joshua. Her smile reached deep into her large brown eyes, fringed in long, black lashes. The beat of his heart accelerated. He gripped his fork tighter.

"I agree with my son, Lizzy. But if I remember correctly, you make a great lasagna, too." Darcy's shoulder-length blond hair fell forward and she pushed it behind her ears.

With the conversation turning to favorite foods, Joshua sat back, watching the exchange at the table. The lively gleam in Darcy's eyes made her whole face light up. He tried to picture her breaking in a yearling, but couldn't. She was petite, not more than five foot two.

When Lizzy served sliced peaches and ice cream for dessert, Sean snapped his fingers and said, "I've got the perfect name for the new filly. Peaches."

"Not a bad name, son." Shamus frowned at Lizzy, who had handed him a bowl of peaches without the vanilla ice cream.

When Joshua's cell phone rang, everyone shifted their attention to him.

"Sorry." He retrieved his phone from his pocket and checked the message. Tension whipped down his length as he surged to his feet. "I have to leave. There's a fire at the Coleman farm."

Darcy's eyes widened and she came to her feet too, her napkin floating to the carpet. "A barn?"

A new tension descended in the room. "Yes," Joshua said as he headed toward the door.

Chapter Three

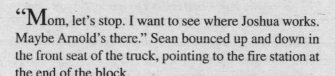

"Mom, let's stop. I want to see where Joshua works. Maybe Arnold's there." Sean bounced up and down in the front seat of the truck, pointing to the fire station at the end of the block.

"Hon, I still need to pick up some things at the store and there's a lot to do back at the farm."

"Pleease, Mom."

Pausing at the stop sign, Darcy chanced a look at her son. The eagerness in his expression shoved away all her doubts. Just because she had thought about Joshua Markham several times in the past forty-eight hours—okay, more than several times—didn't mean she couldn't pay him a visit, then go her merry way. "All right. But we can't stay long. And if he's busy, we'll need to leave."

"Sure." Sean stretched his neck to get a better look at the fire station as Darcy pulled into the driveway and parked behind the building.

"Hon, he might not be here."

"He is."

Suspicion began to form in her mind. "How do you know?"

Sean ducked his head to the side and studied the scenery out the side window as though fascinated with the brick wall several feet from the truck.

"Sean."

"Uh—" He stared down at his hands fidgeting in his lap. "I called him this morning." Her son's voice was barely audible.

"Sean, you know better than to bother a busy man."

He lifted his head, turning his appealing look on her. "But, Mom, he told me I could play with Arnold. I wanted to find out when."

"That doesn't mean you have an open invitation to visit him at work or to call him anytime you want."

"Yes, I do." His grin split his face. "He invited me this morning. Said I was welcome to come by anytime they were there."

"Only *after* you called." Darcy gripped the steering wheel and thought about backing out and escaping before anyone saw them. Her dream about the fire last night was filled with the image of the smoke and fog parting and Joshua walking toward her. Everything had dimmed except the man in the fire gear striding toward her with exhaustion evident in every line of his handsome face. Confidence had marked his stance as he'd come to a stop in front of her. His blue eyes had gleamed in the early morning light, drawing her toward him— dangerously close.

The flashback to the previous dream made beads of perspiration pop out on her upper lip. Darcy brushed them away. What am I doing? *I have no business thinking about Joshua Markham in any terms other than as a firefighter and an acquaintance.* She started to switch on the engine and leave before anyone knew they were there. She would find some excuse to give her son.

Too late. Joshua waved from the door and strode toward them.

"See. He's expecting us."

Darcy wanted to hide. She felt the heat suffuse her cheeks as the man walked to the truck, a smile of greeting on his face. The first thing she thought about was the dusty jeans and the old worn shirt she wore. Why hadn't she changed before coming into town? Why did she care? Her record with men was no good. She just had to think about her husband and father to confirm that.

Joshua stopped on her side of the truck, his face framed in her window, only a few inches from her. She rolled down the window and forced a smile to her lips. "Is this a bad time to come?" *Please let it be,* she silently added, even as she responded to his heart-melting grin, her pulse accelerating.

"It's been quiet around here."

"That's good" was all she could think to say with the man dominating her space, his musky scent surrounding her.

"Yeah, we feel the same way."

"Where's Arnold?" Sean asked, unbuckling his seat belt.

"He's in the station. Come on in and meet the rest of the guys."

Sean hopped from the truck before Darcy could say anything. Joshua opened her door, and she slid out, glad to see her legs would support her weight. Her son ran ahead while she and Joshua walked at a leisurely pace toward the building.

"I checked with my friend about a puppy for Sean. It's fine with him. In fact, he can have the pick of the litter."

"How much are the puppies?"

"Free. He just wants to give the puppies good homes."

Darcy halted, causing Joshua to do the same. "What aren't you telling me?"

He stuffed his hands into his pockets. "I told him I didn't want the pick of the litter."

"So Sean gets it instead. I can pay for a puppy. I know teachers don't get rich teaching, but—"

"I wanted to do this for Sean."

"Why?"

"I can remember my first dog when I was growing up. Lady was so special to me. I want Sean to experience that."

"But—"

Joshua held up his hand to stop her protest. "If you saw my house and the animals I have, you wouldn't say anything. I don't need to take on another pet."

"How many do you have?"

"Three dogs besides Arnold, two cats, a rabbit and an aquarium full of fish."

"Don't tell Sean. He'll be begging to come over."

"I've never bought one of those animals. Either people give them to me because they don't want them anymore or they are left in my yard."

He was a large, muscular man in a dangerous profession, but underneath everything he was a softie, taking in strays. There had been times when married to Clay that she'd felt like a stray, wandering from city to city looking for a permanent home. She was glad now that she and Sean had one in Panama City. This spring had been the beginning of their second year there.

Sean stood at the door to the fire station, waiting for them. He hopped from one foot to the other. "Come *on,* Mom," he finally shouted when he couldn't contain his impatience any longer.

"Do you want me to tell him about the puppy now?" Joshua said in a low voice.

"You might wait until later or he'll want you to leave your job and show him the puppy."

"I'm off on Sunday. How about after church? We can leave after the eleven o'clock service, pick up something to eat for lunch, then go to Ned's. Sean can pick out the puppy he wants."

Darcy didn't say anything for a few seconds. She'd made plans to start going to church again with Lizzy. She'd gotten out of the habit when married to Clay.

They had moved so often it had become difficult to find a place to worship where she was comfortable—at least, that was the excuse she'd given herself over the years.

"I'm sorry. I'm assuming you'll be going to church while you're home. I can meet you at Ned's place if you want."

"No. Lizzy mentioned something to me the other day."

"You can come with Lizzy, and then I can bring you and Sean home later. I should have the results back from the lab by then and I promised your father a report on what I found."

Sean danced around. "Mom! I've got to *go*."

Joshua chuckled. "I guess we'd better get inside."

"It was that pop he drank on the way into town."

Joshua reached around Sean and pulled the door open. "The rest room is down the hall on the left."

Her son shot down the corridor and disappeared into the bathroom. They waited by the entrance until he came out into the hall. He headed straight for them with determination on his face.

"Where's Arnold?"

"Probably watching TV."

"He watches TV?"

"Yep, I'm afraid so. Nasty habit he's gotten into. The last time I saw him he was in the living area in front of the set." Joshua gestured to the right.

Sean darted ahead of them into a large room with several couches and chair. A table that sat twelve was off to one side in a spacious kitchen of gleaming stainless steel. Arnold was where Joshua had left him, perched before the big-screen television set, his head resting on his front paws.

"He really *does* watch TV," Darcy said in astonishment.

While Sean kneeled next to the black Lab, Joshua chuckled. "Like I said, a really nasty habit he developed. He likes the noise, and when a dog appears he begins to bark, which doesn't always sit well with the other guys who are trying to watch the show."

"What does he do when a cat appears?" Darcy watched her son rub the length of Arnold's back, then bury his face in his fur.

The dog rolled over, his tail wagging.

"He loves cats. His best buddy is Ringo, a white male cat that found me about two years ago and adopted us. When we're at home, they are usually inseparable."

"Hasn't Arnold heard a cat is a dog's enemy?"

"Apparently not."

An older man came into the room, Joshua introduced him to Darcy and Sean as his captain. When he left, another man, younger, entered and waved at Darcy.

"Joshua said something about you and your son coming to visit this morning." Glen hugged her. "I haven't seen you since right after high school graduation."

"We went to school together since kindergarten," Darcy said to Joshua, then turned back to Glen. "I heard you married your high school sweetheart."

"Nancy and I will have been married ten years come this July. How's your father doing? I'm sorry about the fire at the farm."

"He's the same. Thinks he can single-handedly do everything around the farm."

"That sounds like Shamus. Well, it's my turn to make lunch so I'd better get going before I have seven guys breathing down my neck." Glen made his way into the kitchen area and opened the refrigerator.

"Sean, would you like to go on a tour of the station?" Joshua asked.

Her son glanced up. "Can Arnold come too?"

"Sure, if you can get him to move from the TV set."

Sean leaped to his feet and patted his leg. "Come on, Arnold."

The black Lab lumbered to his feet and nudged Sean's hand so he would continue rubbing him behind the ear.

"I think your son has a gift with animals."

Darcy thought of all the times Sean had wanted a pet and Clay had refused to let him. She thought of how her son had taken to the farm as though he'd grown up there, doing chores, helping take care of the horses and other animals. Her throat closed. She should have brought Sean to the farm sooner. For her son's sake, she should have put her past with her father behind her. It had taken a crisis with her father to get her back home. But the minute she had stepped on Shamrock land, all her insecurities, doubts and guilt had flooded her, as though she'd never left ten years ago.

"Wait up, Darcy."

Darcy turned to see her best friend from high school

hurrying toward her from the back of the church. For a few seconds she lost Jesse Bradshaw in the crowd, which was not unusual since her friend was only five feet tall. Darcy stepped to the side to allow the other parishioners to pass while she waited.

"I should berate you, Darcy O'Brien, for not coming by to see me, but I know you've had your hands full with your father's illness and the fire. I'm sorry." Jesse Bradshaw hugged Darcy. "I'm missed you." She pulled back to get a good look at Darcy. "You haven't changed a bit."

Darcy laughed. "I've missed you, Jesse, and you *have* changed." Her friend had lost twenty or so pounds, and her long brown hair was now short and feathered about her pixie-like features. The only thing the same was her green eyes—clear and sparkling with humor. Darcy turned to the side. "This is my son, Sean."

Shaking Sean's hand, Jesse said, "My son, Nate, is around here somewhere. You two will have to get together. Darcy, I'll call you this week. Let's get together for lunch. I want to know everything that's happened to you in the last ten years. E-mails just don't tell me what's really going on with you." Jesse fell into line with them to speak with the reverend.

"There's Joshua. He's waiting for us by his truck. Come on, Mom." Sean tugged on her arm.

"Joshua Markham?" Jesse asked, one brow quirked.

"Yes, he's helping Sean get a puppy." Darcy leaned toward her friend. "And that is *all,* so don't get any ideas."

Jesse held up her hand. "Who, me? Never."

Moving forward in the line, Darcy smiled at Reverend Collins and shook his hand. "I enjoyed your sermon." Out of the corner of her eye she could see her son dancing about.

"It's good to see you back home, Darcy. Don't be a stranger."

Darcy pulled Sean to her side. "And this eager young man is my son, Sean."

The reverend held out his hand. "I hope we'll get to see more of you this summer."

Sean contained his enthusiasm long enough to straighten and shake the man's hand. "Joshua introduced me to a couple of the boys in his Sunday school class. One lives down the road from Grandpa."

"That must be Brad Anderson."

"Yep." Sean glanced up at Darcy. "Can we go now? I don't want to be late."

After saying her goodbyes to Reverend Collins and Jesse, Darcy allowed her son to drag her toward Joshua. As they approached, Darcy's heart increased its beat, aware that her friend was probably watching every move she made. She didn't dare look back at Jesse and encourage her in any way.

Darcy turned her full focus on the man before her. The sight of Joshua in black slacks with a sky-blue short-sleeved shirt and a striped tie was just as compelling as the image of him in his fire gear or navy-blue firefighter's uniform. The bright sun beamed down on her, but that wasn't the reason she perspired more than usual. The warm greeting in Joshua's eyes did strange things to her. Her stomach flip-flopped; her pulse quickened.

"Are you ready, Sean?" Joshua asked, swinging open the passenger door of his red truck.

"Yes."

"I thought we would grab something to eat, then go to Ned's."

The wide grin on her son's face fell.

"Or, we could go to Ned's first, then eat," Joshua amended when he saw Sean's crestfallen expression.

"Yes!" Sean hopped up into the cab.

"I can't believe he's turning down a meal. That just goes to show you how important this puppy is to Sean." Darcy followed her son into the truck, relieved she wasn't pressed up against Joshua.

He shut the door and leaned forward, his head framed in the open window. "You understand, Sean, you won't be able to take the puppy home for a few more weeks."

"Can I visit my puppy?"

"I don't think Ned will mind—if it's okay with your mother."

Sean sent her a beseeching look.

"We'll work something out," she said.

Her son breathed a deep sigh of relief while Joshua rounded the front of the truck and slid behind the steering wheel.

"Actually, Ned lives about halfway to your farm on Old State Road, not too far from Sweetwater Lake."

"Maybe I could walk to his place."

"No way, young man," said Darcy. "When you get your chores done, I'll drive you. No walking along that highway."

"But, Mom—"

Joshua backed out of the parking space. "I've had a few near misses out on Old State Road. Some people think its straightaway is an invitation to race. Not a safe place to be."

Again Sean sighed, but he remained quiet.

In a short time Darcy had begun to notice the influence Joshua had over her son. For a boy hungry for male attention, Joshua was a wonderful role model. But what was going to happen when they returned to Panama City in August? She hated disappointing her son. For years he had tried to get his father interested in what he was doing, but Clay had hardly ever been around. When they'd been in the same room, it had been as though they were strangers.

As they drove toward Ned's, her son thankfully kept up a running commentary about the Sunday school class he'd joined that day, the one Joshua taught. Sean described each of the boys he'd met and gave a rundown on their likes and dislikes. She was glad he had been readily accepted by his peers, especially Brad Anderson and Nate Bradshaw, Jesse's son. Darcy relaxed and listened to Sean and Joshua.

Fifteen minutes later Joshua drove through an opened gate and down a gravel road that ended in front of a one-story, white, wooden house with an old brown barn nearby. "He's probably in the barn."

"Does he raise horses like Grandpa?" Sean exited the truck on Joshua's side.

That gave Darcy a chance to take her time and allow the two guys to go ahead of her. She heard Joshua say, "No, he takes in strays like I do. He's a firefighter at the station where I work. He doesn't have a lot of land, just a few acres. But I must say, he has more room than I do. I'm running out of places to put my animals."

Dressed in a plaid short-sleeved shirt, a man who appeared to be in his forties came out of the barn. He brushed some dust from his jeans and adjusted his navy-blue ball cap. "Right on time. I just got through feeding the animals."

Sean raced forward. "Where are the puppies?"

Ned placed a hand on the boy's shoulder and led him into the barn. Joshua waited for her by the entrance.

"I think your son is excited."

"A small understatement."

"I'm glad he enjoyed this morning. How did you like the adult class?"

"Lizzy and Jesse took me under their wing. I didn't realize there were so many new people since I last attended."

"When was that?"

"Over ten years ago."

"You never had time to come with Lizzy when you visited?"

Darcy stepped into the coolness of the barn, the familiar scents of leather, dirt and hay drifting to her.

"This is the first time I've been home since I got married."

When Joshua didn't say anything for several heartbeats, Darcy felt compelled to add, "We were out of the country for half that time."

"You don't owe me an explanation."

"I know, but I didn't realize it was that long until I came home. Lizzy was quick to point that out to me."

"Not your father?"

Sean's laughter floated to her. She looked toward her son in the middle of a pen with six puppies crawling all over him. "No, my relationship with my father has been strained for years." She wasn't sure why she told Joshua that, but for some reason it felt right to confide in him, which surprised her, but he was easy to talk to and she suspected he didn't judge a person.

"You returned home when he needed you the most."

She paused a few yards from Sean so he wouldn't hear her reply. "I'm not sure my father needs me right now. He is trying to continue doing everything himself even though he is supposed to be resting and learning to take life a little easier."

"Like the fire?"

"I finally convinced him to let me take care of stabling the mares. But I don't think he rested much. He had all the book work done when I returned to the office later. But I guess sitting at a desk is better than running around the farm."

"Sometimes it's hard for a person to accept help or to even ask for it."

"That definitely describes my father."

"My father could be stubborn at times, but…" His voice faded into silence as he glanced away.

"But what?"

"I'd trade anything to have those times back. I miss our…lively discussions."

"It sounds like you had a good relationship with your father."

His intense gaze swung back to her. "It wasn't perfect, but yes, we had a good relationship."

How could she tell Joshua that she would give anything to have a good relationship with her father? How could she tell him that her father had been disappointed she wasn't a male and that she was an only child? She would never forget the time she'd overheard her parents arguing and her mother shouting at her father that she was glad they hadn't had any more children. He didn't deserve to have the son he'd always wanted, that he would have to settle for passing his farm on to a daughter. She'd run from the house and hidden in the loft of the barn, crying until there were no tears left inside. Her mother's words had explained a lot to her— her father's demands to be perfect, her father's coldness and distance. But still, it hurt to this day.

Joshua's expression softened. Darcy closed her eyes, afraid the anguish she experienced every time she remembered that day was evident in them. His finger brushed across her cheek.

"You're crying." He captured her hand and laced his fingers through hers. "Some say I'm a good listener."

Through a sheen she viewed the tenderness in his expression and wanted to go into the comfort she knew she would find in his arms. With a supreme effort she held herself back, because that wasn't her. She'd already told Joshua more than she shared with others. She attempted a smile that wavered about the corners of her mouth, then vanished.

"I think the trauma of the fire is finally catching up with me."

His gaze ensnared hers as though he were delving into her mind to read her deepest thoughts, those she kept hidden from the world.

"I know we don't know each other well," he said, "but if I—"

"Mom! Joshua! Aren't you coming?"

Darcy blinked, tugged her hand from Joshua's and started for her son. Joshua's gaze bore into her back and her steps quickened. She had been so close to telling him about her childhood—and that frightened her. She hadn't even told her husband how hard it had been growing up with warring parents and a mother who— She wouldn't think about the past. Hadn't she learned that reliving it only brought her pain?

This time when she smiled, it stayed in place. She'd become good at putting up a front for her son's sake. She entered the pen and kneeled next to Sean. "Have you decided on one yet?"

"I can't decide between this one—" he held up a male black Lab "—or this one." Scooping up the puppy into his lap, he showed her a smaller female with a lighter mark on its brow. "I think she's the runt. Which one do you like the most?"

"Son, it's your choice."

"Yeah, but what if I choose wrong?"

That innocent question brought a lump to her throat. She'd made some wrong choices that she wished she could do over, but life wasn't like that. She swallowed and replied, "Making mistakes is how we learn, but I don't think you can go wrong picking between these two adorable puppies."

The female nudged Sean's hand while the male licked him, then began gnawing on his finger. "Joshua, what do you think?"

Joshua chuckled. "I agree with your mother. It's your call."

Her son then turned his attention to Ned, who shook his head and said, "No, partner, you're on your own."

Sean's face brightened. "Mom, how about taking both? I have some money saved. I could buy the other one."

"I think, Sweetie, for your first pet we should stick to having only one." Darcy straightened, aware of Joshua standing right behind her. She always seemed to know where he was in relation to her. That shook her. "You don't have to make up your mind right this minute."

"No, why don't you play with them for a while? I have some iced tea up at the house. We'll be sitting on the porch when you're ready." Ned headed out of the barn.

Darcy backed away. She watched her son bury his

face in the fur of first the female, then the male. She thought about the small yard they had in Panama City and knew one big dog was all they could handle.

"It's tough making that kind of decision," Joshua murmured as they walked from the barn.

"If the dogs were going to be smaller, we might be able to have two." She peered back once more to see Sean lying on the ground with both puppies on his chest. He was talking to them.

"It's hard setting limits."

"As a parent all I want to do is protect my son from the world and any problems that might arise."

"Impossible."

"I know." *Better than most,* she added silently, remembering being caught between two parents who had fought all the time, often using her as a referee. She had promised herself when she married that her marriage would be different. It had been, because she had given in to her husband's wishes instead of standing up for what she believed in.

She didn't believe anymore that it was possible for two people to be equal partners in a marriage. And so she would never marry again.

Chapter Four

"Mom, I don't know which puppy to take. I liked playing with both of them," Sean said, popping his last french fry into his mouth. "What do you think, Joshua?"

"Listen to your heart. You can't go wrong."

Yes, you can, Darcy thought, remembering her marriage. She'd been in love with Clay, but over the years his indifference had eroded her feelings until they had been two strangers living in the same household—much like her parents. Now she relied on her head rather than her heart when it came to important matters. Much safer.

Sean downed the rest of his soft drink. "Then I think I want the runt of the litter. She needs me."

Darcy cocked her head. "Why do you say that?"

"Because she's small like me. Probably no one will pick her. She'll need a home and someone to love her."

Her heart twisted at the pain behind her son's words. She knew why he felt that way. Clay. Her husband over the years had made more than one comment about how small their son was. Clay had wanted Sean involved in sports and hadn't been sure if that would be possible.

"Size isn't important, Sean. It's what's inside that counts," Joshua said as he gathered up their trash and stacked it on the tray. "Until I was fifteen, I was several inches smaller than most guys in my class. Then all of a sudden I began to grow and didn't stop until I was in my early twenties. I more than made up for my lack of height as a child." Joshua slid from the booth and rose, all six feet and a few inches.

Sean craned his neck and looked at Joshua. "You think I'll be tall like you?"

"Can't say. You'll be as tall as you need to be."

Darcy slipped from the booth, followed by her son who beamed from ear to ear. Seeing Sean with Joshua only reconfirmed that her son needed a man's influence in his life. Clay hadn't been around much for Sean, and a mother just couldn't offer certain things for a boy.

"I still want the girl puppy. Maybe one day she can have a litter. I could sell all the puppies except one."

"Hold it, young man. I'm only agreeing to one dog at the moment."

"Aw, Mom, I don't mean right away. That'll be *years* from now."

"Then I'll call Ned and tell him that's your choice." Joshua held the door open for Darcy and Sean.

"Will you ask him if I can come visit her tomorrow? I want her to get to know me so she won't be so scared when she leaves her mother."

"How do you expect to get over there?" Darcy asked while walking toward Joshua's truck in the parking lot of the fast-food restaurant.

Sean's smile grew. "You?"

Remembering how demanding her father had been about her first horse, she never wanted her son to feel he couldn't live up to his parent's expectations. "Only after you do your chores. When you're responsible for animals, their needs come before yours. If you want that horse this summer, you have to show Grandpa you can take care of it."

"It's a deal."

Joshua unlocked his truck, and Sean climbed into the front seat, followed by Darcy. Joshua backed out of the parking space and waited to pull out into traffic.

"Joshua, can I see Arnold today?"

Joshua glanced at Darcy, a question in his eyes. She shrugged, realizing she'd like to see where he lived. Did his house fit the man? She could tell a lot by a person's surroundings.

"Sure, if you promise to play catch with him. That's his favorite thing, next to TV."

"Yes!" In his excitement Sean bounced on the seat.

Ten minutes later Joshua pulled into the driveway of a one-story white cottage with a beautiful, manicured yard. Red and yellow impatiens lined the bed in front of a rock garden surrounding a century-old oak tree that shaded the house. A bird bath with several cardinals in it graced the middle of the rock garden.

Darcy followed the round stepping stones from the

driveway to the porch. Off to the side sat a white wicker table and two comfortable-looking chairs with striped forest-green-and-tan cushions. A perfect place to enjoy a cup of coffee in the early morning, she thought while Joshua unlocked his house.

For a few seconds she pictured herself sitting in one of the chairs with Joshua in the other, discussing a favorite book or a movie they'd seen. He would laugh at something witty she'd said and she would—whoa. Where had that fantasy come from? She hurried inside before her thoughts took her any further.

Darcy hadn't been sure what to expect, but when she walked into Joshua's house, surprise flickered through her. One small brown dog, a mix of four or five breeds, bounded from the back of the house, yelping and jumping into the air. A large white cat stirred from the navy-blue sofa, stretched, then lumbered toward them.

"Missy, sit."

The brown mutt immediately obeyed Joshua's command. The cat weaved in and out of her legs, rubbing his body against her while purring. Another smaller cat, various shades of gray, came from the hallway at a lazy pace.

"You *do* have a lot of animals," Darcy said, bending over to pet the white cat with two different colored eyes.

"What can I say? I can't turn away a stray."

Sean kneeled on the hardwood floor next to Missy and stroked her. "Where's Arnold?"

"Out back with my other two dogs. Come on. I'll

show you." Joshua started forward with Sean next to him. Joshua paused at the entrance into the kitchen and glanced back at Darcy. "Make yourself at home. I'll only be a sec."

While he was gone, Darcy scanned the living room, a large open room with a high ceiling. Beautifully carved built-in bookcases, filled with books and Indian pottery, graced one whole wall, while the others were painted a rich, deep burgundy. The room should have been dark, but the large windows with plantation shutters along the front of the house allowed sunlight to pour in. The hardwood floor in the entryway continued throughout the living room with one area rug of burgundy-and-navy between the couch and two cushioned chairs with ottomans. On the massive coffee table sat a large, black leather-bound Bible that probably had been handed down for generations.

Comfort came to mind as Darcy looked around. And a sense of warmth. A lot of care had gone into Joshua's home. The man was continually surprising her. Clay had never wanted anything to do with their houses. She'd always thought it was because they had moved so much that he had found it hard to become attached to any one place. But in reality, her husband had never viewed their houses as home.

"Grab a seat. I'll get us something to drink."

Joshua's voice startled Darcy. "I didn't hear you come in."

"Sorry. I'll whistle my approach next time."

"No, you just caught me thinking."

"About what?"

"Your house. I love it. I can tell a lot of thought went into it."

A shadow clouded Joshua's eyes. His mouth firmed into a hard line. "It did." He turned away, a rigidity to his stance. "I've got some iced tea."

He was gone before Darcy could say anything. She wondered about the sudden tension that had sparked the air. She made her way to the couch and sat. The white cat jumped up and lay in her lap. Darcy buried her fingers in his soft fur and rubbed, still pondering the change in Joshua's disposition.

"If Ringo's bothering you, just put him on the floor. He loves people and likes to make himself at home in their laps," Joshua said, coming toward her carrying two tall glasses.

She saw none of the earlier, tense expression. Maybe she had imagined it. After all, she'd given him a compliment. But some people were uncomfortable with compliments. Taking an iced tea from him, Darcy sipped, relishing the cold drink.

"I've never seen such beautiful craftsmanship before. Did these bookcases come with the house?" Darcy placed her glass on a coaster on the coffee table, wanting to recapture the ease they'd had when they'd talked earlier.

"No, I made them."

Her gaze shifted to him. "You did? How long did it take?"

"Months, working on my days off."

"Have you done other pieces of furniture?" Such craft had obviously gone into his work. There were many facets to this man.

His mouth tightened into a frown. "Yes. My bed."

Darcy almost asked to see it, but an undercurrent flowed between them as though she had journeyed into forbidden territory. Again she felt the tension take hold of Joshua and wondered about it. "You're gifted. If you ever want to stop being a firefighter, you could make a living carving furniture."

"It's just a hobby." Joshua took several large swallows of his tea, draining half the glass.

"You're a man full of interesting surprises. Most don't go to this much trouble when it's just them living alone."

His grip was so tight that his knuckles whitened on his glass. "It wasn't supposed to be just me."

"Oh?"

"I was engaged once."

"What happened?" Her teeth dug into her lower lip.

Joshua carefully put his drink on a coaster, his gaze lifting to hers. For a few seconds she glimpsed pain, until he veiled the expression and averted his look. She shouldn't have asked. She'd overstepped her bounds with the question, but she wanted to know everything about him. He interested her—more than she should allow, she realized.

She was about to rise when he finally said, "It's not really a big secret. In fact, the whole town knows. My fiancée left me at the altar last year because she was having another man's baby."

His words caught her completely by surprise and wrenched her heart. How awful. But she suspected he didn't want to hear those words. She let the silence grow while he wrestled with his demons. The clenching of his jaw and the stiffening of his body spoke of the emotions gripping him.

"I'd spent six months getting this house ready for Carol. I'd wanted everything perfect. The problem was, while I was lovingly carving the bookcases and bed, she was seeing another man. I..." His voice trailed off into the silence. He swallowed hard and reestablished eye contact with Darcy. "I should have spent the time with Carol. But I love working with my hands and this—" he swept his arm to indicate the whole house "—was my way of expressing my love for her."

"She didn't want to help?"

"She did a little, but she didn't like physical work. Computers were more her thing. She would spend hours in front of one. I need to be up and working. Sitting for too long drives me crazy."

"About the only time I sit is to read a good book. That's what I do when I have the time."

The corners of Joshua's mouth lifted in a lopsided grin that eased the tension momentarily. "Since you're a librarian, that makes sense."

Darcy chuckled. "I guess I'd better like books or I'd be surrounded by something I don't like every day at work." She shifted on the couch, leaning back against the cushion. "Does Carol live in Sweetwater?"

"Yes. She married the man and they have—" he cleared his throat "—a seven-month-old son."

"Do you see her much?" There was a part of her that was shocked at the boldness of her questions; the other part wanted to know the answers, wanted to know Joshua.

"Not often. She used to go to the same church, but now goes to a different one across town."

"I'm sorry things didn't work out, but maybe what happened was for the best. If you aren't right for each other, it's better to discover that before the marriage rather than after." *Like I did,* Darcy thought, folding her arms over her chest.

"I keep telling myself that. The worst part about the whole situation is that it makes me doubt my judgment. How could I be so wrong about Carol? We'd known each other for years—dated for three of them."

How many times had she asked herself that very question concerning Clay? "Maybe you didn't see the true Carol. People have a way of putting up a front. The problem is, that front won't last forever. A person's true character comes out in the end."

Joshua picked up his drink and finished it in several swallows. "Speaking from experience?"

She wished she could tell him. But she wasn't used to sharing much of herself with anyone. She'd tried with Clay and he'd rejected her feelings. Between her experiences with her father and Clay, she'd learned to keep everything buried deep inside. "I was just making an observation. I'm sure everyone has dealt with people who aren't always who they seem to be."

He studied her. The silence in the room stretched to an uncomfortable level. Darcy crossed her legs, then uncrossed them.

"I suppose you're right," he finally said.

His words cut through the silence, but did nothing to relieve the tension building in Darcy. She pushed herself to her feet. "I probably should check on Sean, make sure he's staying out of trouble. It's been awfully quiet for the past twenty minutes."

"He's got three dogs to play with. When I left him, he was smiling from ear to ear while they licked him."

"That's my son. Give him an animal and he can entertain himself for hours."

"Then Sean and I have something in common."

Darcy followed Joshua through the kitchen, a sunny, cheerful room decorated in yellows and reds with dark walnut cabinets polished to a rich sheen. The tan tiled countertops and floor contrasted with the plaid wallpaper, complimenting each other.

When she stepped out onto the deck, she was taken by its beauty. A rose garden graced the east side, while a garden full of wildflowers stood along the west fence. A pond fed by a fountain was the focal point in the rock garden along the deck. Several maple trees with two stone benches under them presented a place to seek shade in the heat of summer.

"Do you like to do yard work, too?"

Joshua glanced around, his gaze touching each garden. "Yes. I do draw the line at housework, however. I have someone come in once a week to clean for me."

"Frankly, I don't know when you would have time to do that anyway. You do like to be busy."

"There're so many things I want to do and so little time."

"Mom, watch this," Sean shouted from beneath a maple tree.

Her son held up a Frisbee and sent it sailing through the air. Arnold leaped up and caught it, then trotted back to Sean.

"Isn't he great?"

Two more dogs, one a cross between a collie and a German shepherd and the other with a lot of Chow in him, vied for Sean's attention. He tossed a ball for each of them to fetch.

"Where do you draw the line at taking in strays?" Darcy asked, turning slightly so she faced Joshua.

Sunlight danced in his blue eyes. "I haven't found that point yet. I usually manage to locate homes for my strays, but if I can't, I keep them until I find one. Every once in a while one of the strays touches me in a certain way and I end up keeping him for a pet."

"Hence the four dogs and two cats?"

He nodded, silent laughter making his eyes sparkle. "That's one of the reasons I fell in love with this house. The yard is so big."

"You know, when we return to Panama City I'm gonna have a hard time with Sean. He'll probably start wanting a larger house so he can have more pets. I won't be surprised if he doesn't start finding strays. Joshua Markham, you have made quite an impression on my son in the short time we've known you."

He straightened, satisfaction stamped on his features. "I aim to please."

That was the problem. He was pleasing to look at, pleasing to be around. She had no intention of getting serious about a man after her marriage to Clay, but she was finding that harder and harder to remember the more she was with Joshua.

"Why didn't Grandpa come with us?" Sean asked as he hopped from the car and started for the church.

"He was tired and thought he would go to bed early tonight." Darcy trailed behind her son with Lizzy at her side.

"Maybe he'll come on Sunday with us." Seeing Nate Bradshaw, Sean hurried into the building.

Lizzy stopped on the sidewalk to catch her breath. "You and I both know your father won't come on Sunday or next Wednesday night. He hasn't stepped foot in church since the day of your mother's funeral."

"I know. Maybe Sean can do what you and I couldn't—get Dad to come to church."

Lizzy shook her head. "I've been trying for the past thirteen years to no avail. He's unusually quiet about his reasons behind stopping, which in itself is a mystery. Your father is rarely quiet about anything."

As well Darcy knew. She had been on more than one occasion at the other end of her father's sharp tongue and biting opinions. She held one of the double glass doors open for Lizzy, who carried a large casserole dish for the Wednesday-night potluck dinner and church service. While Lizzy headed toward the kitchen, Darcy was letting the door close when a woman about her age with a young girl in a wheelchair approached. Smiling at the woman and child, Darcy stepped to the side to allow them into the building. The young girl, her face with an ashen complexion, grinned up at Darcy.

"Hi, I'm Darcy O'Brien."

"I'm Crystal."

Darcy glanced at the tall, slightly overweight woman with shoulder-length light brown hair and hazel eyes pushing Crystal's wheelchair.

"And I'm Crystal's mother, Tanya. Lizzy said something about Shamus Flanaghan's daughter and grandson coming home for the summer." The woman smiled, two dimples appearing in her cheeks.

"That would be me," Darcy said, responding to the upbeat, enthusiastic tone in the woman's voice and the happy expression on her face.

"Well, it's a pleasure meeting you. Lizzy has been such a dear to me and my family since the accident." Tanya started toward the rec hall, maneuvering the wheelchair around people in the foyer. "This is our first outing in a long time. Crystal's been dying to see her friends."

Inside the large room with rows of tables set for dinner, Tanya wheeled Crystal toward a group of children standing around the piano. The music director was play-

ing and the kids were singing. When a song ended,
everyone greeted Crystal, a couple of the girls hugging
her. Tanya backed away and stood next to Darcy.

The woman blew out a relieved breath. "I'm glad
that's over with."

"What?"

"Crystal was anxious about this first meeting."

"You said something about an accident. What happened?"

Tanya frowned, the lines on her forehead deepening
into grooves. "She was taking a riding lesson when her
horse got spooked and bolted. She fell and injured her
spine. The doctors say she'll never walk again."

Darcy remembered her own falls from a horse and
shivered. "I'm sorry." The words seemed inadequate.

"Crystal's got a great attitude. She'll be okay. That's
more than I can say about her father."

The children finished singing and began moving toward the couch area with the youth minister. Tanya
rushed forward to push her daughter. Darcy headed toward the kitchen to help Lizzy with the dinner setup.

"I see you met Tanya Bolton and Crystal," Lizzy said,
handing Darcy a stack of plates to put on the serving table.

"Yes. When did Crystal have her riding accident?"

"Last fall. Tragic. Tom, her father, has been a hard
man to live with. I try to help as much as I can, but he
is so angry. Tanya had enough to cope with before the
accident. Now I don't know how she does it."

Darcy came back to pick up another stack of plates.
"Money problems?"

Lizzy nodded. "Crystal's accident has been very hard on the family, financially as well as emotionally. Tanya needs all the friends she can get right now." She pinned Darcy with a worried expression. "And your prayers."

"That I can give." Darcy peered through the door into the rec hall and found the woman standing by her daughter, listening to the youth minister. Her heart went out to Tanya Bolton. If something like that happened to Sean, she wasn't sure how she would handle it.

Darcy's gaze shifted away and lit upon Joshua speaking with the reverend. Her heartbeat responded with a quicker pace. He looked good to the eyes, Darcy thought, taking in Joshua dressed casually in a pair of tan slacks and navy-blue polo shirt. The blue brought out the color of his eyes.

She recalled the pain she'd seen reflected in those eyes when he'd talked about his ex-fiancée. She, too, had been through a difficult relationship, so she felt a kinship with Joshua. That was all she could allow, however. In a few months she and Sean would return to Panama City where their home was. Sweetwater wasn't home anymore. Sometimes she wondered if it ever really had been.

Joshua caught her looking at him. A smile lit his eyes, the lines at the corners of them deepening. A dimple appeared at his mouth and held her attention for a few seconds before she averted her gaze.

She turned back toward Lizzy. "What else do you need me to do?"

"We just need to get the dishes on the table and then we're ready to eat."

"Sounds good to me. I haven't eaten since breakfast."

"Can I help you two?"

Joshua's question brought her around to face him. "Sure. As you can see, we have a lot of food." Darcy waved toward all the dishes on the counter.

Side by side she and Joshua worked to put the food out on the long serving table while Lizzy put finishing touches on some of the dishes. Seeing Joshua here this evening added a bounce to Darcy's walk, as though his presence completed the night. She shouldn't feel that way. She had every intention of leaving Sweetwater when the summer was over. She and her father couldn't stay in the same town for long. She didn't want to fall into the same old pattern she'd been in while growing up, and even while married to Clay. She was just discovering who Darcy O'Brien really was.

"I'm glad to see you here tonight." Joshua's deep, rich voice cut into her thoughts, bringing her back to the present.

"You are?"

"Yes. I was going to call you tomorrow. Ned says that Sean can have his puppy a little earlier than usual. After your son's visit the other day, he decided that Sean would be a great owner and there wasn't any reason to wait another week."

"Have you told Sean yet?"

"No, I wanted to run it by you first."

"If I know my son, he'll want to go over to Ned's tomorrow morning before the sun rises."

Joshua laughed. "Afraid he'll have to wait a little. Ned doesn't go off duty until the afternoon."

"Sean will be beside himself. Dad has arranged for him to have a horse. He'll be riding him for the first time tomorrow morning. Are you off?"

He nodded. "Why?"

"This would be a good time for you to go riding with us. Remember you said you wanted to ride more? Well, I'm giving you the perfect excuse to. Then you can go with us to pick up the puppy, since you're the reason we're getting her."

Joshua ran a hand through his hair, thinking. "I have to confess I'm not a good rider. In fact, I'm no kind of rider."

"Then you and Sean will have something in common. Sean's only ridden a few times."

"I hope I don't regret saying yes."

"Joshua Markham, you are a man who takes risks every day in your job. Riding a horse is much easier than fighting fires." Even as she said the last sentence, the image of Crystal in her wheelchair popped into Darcy's mind. She shivered.

"Cold?"

"No, I just thought about Crystal Bolton."

"My point exactly."

"Accidents happen all the time, Joshua. You know that. We can't worry about what might happen. If we did, we'd live in fear all the time and never get up in the morning." Another picture flashed into Darcy's thoughts: her mother locked in her bedroom with the drapes drawn all day long, sleeping and sleeping. She shook the memory from her mind, determined not to journey into the past. "You're a risk taker and you love animals. Riding is perfect for you."

Joshua held up his hand. "Okay. You've convinced me. Why the hard sell?"

"I need a referee. My father is determined to work with Sean and his horse. I'm going along to—" Suddenly she stopped, realizing what she was admitting.

Joshua moved closer, until only inches separated them. "Why are you going along, Darcy?"

"To protect my son." There, she had said it.

"From your father?"

"He taught me to ride but he isn't a very forgiving teacher. But Sean was so excited when Dad said something about it at breakfast, I didn't have the heart to say no. My father is a hard man and Sean is so impressionable." Joshua's scent, with a hint of musk, teased her senses. She should step back. She didn't. "Now that I've told you, do you still want to go?"

His eyes glinted with humor. "Only if you promise to be my teacher."

His look mesmerized her. Her mind blanked—until someone behind her coughed, reminding her that she and Joshua were not alone.

"Hi, Mike. It's good to see you. Do you need something?" Joshua glanced over Darcy's shoulder.

"That spoon in your hand for the casserole if that's not too much of an inconvenience."

Hearing the chuckle in the man's voice, Darcy spun

about, feeling the heat searing her cheeks. "I'm Darcy O'Brien."

"Shamus Flanaghan's daughter?"

"Yes."

"Sorry about that," the man said belligerently before turning to spoon tuna casserole onto his plate.

Stunned, Darcy opened her mouth to say something, thought better of it and snapped her jaws closed. Anger welled up in her. It was one thing for *her* to say something about her father, but she didn't like anyone else to criticize him.

"That's Mike Reynolds, the assistant manager your father fired a few months back."

Joshua's whispered words washed over her, sending a chill down her spine. Again his nearness caused her heart to speed up, something it was doing a lot of around Joshua.

As Mike moved down the line, Darcy stepped away from the serving table to allow others to select their food. "Not a particularly friendly guy."

"I heard the Colemans let him go after the fire. He left in a huff."

"Could he be responsible for the fires?"

Joshua shrugged. "He certainly doesn't stay long at a farm. Soon it will be hard for him to be hired at all. He's garnishing quite a reputation."

"How so?"

"He's too rough with the horses."

The tightness about Joshua's mouth indicated he didn't care for Mike's techniques. "So that was the method my dad didn't like."

"Probably. Mike gets results from his horses, but at a cost."

Her father might have been tough on her when he was raising her, demanding perfection, but he was always gentle with his horses—in fact, any of the animals at the farm. She could remember once when she was a little girl wishing she had been a horse so her father would love her. Hurt, buried deep, rose and threatened to overwhelm her.

"Darcy, are you okay?"

She blinked, focusing on the here and now. Coming home had been tougher than she had thought possible. She slowly gave Joshua a nod, but inside she didn't feel all right. The fragile new life she was building for herself was beginning to unravel and she wasn't sure how to hold it together.

Chapter Five

"**D**ad, are you sure about this?" Darcy asked as she and her father walked toward the barn.

"I'm supposed to start exercising just so long as I don't overdo it. Yes, I'm sure."

"I can teach Sean to ride."

"I want to." Her father gave her a hard look. "I haven't been able to do much else for my only grandchild."

Guilt, just as her father had intended, swamped her. She had allowed her own feelings to get in the way of Sean knowing his grandfather. She'd been wrong, and her father was making sure she knew that.

"So Joshua Markham is coming along. What's going on there?"

Darcy stopped before they reached the barn where Joshua's red truck was parked. "Nothing, Dad, and don't imply there is."

"Mighty defensive, if you ask me."

She huffed and began walking again. "I'm not." This

was going to be a long morning if her father's surly attitude was any indication.

"Mom." Sean raced toward her. "Joshua is a beginner like me."

Darcy caught sight of Joshua standing by his truck, dressed in jeans, boots and a short-sleeved plaid shirt, rubbing his thumb across the pads of his fingers. "I thought it was about time he learned to ride, since this is horse country. What do you think?"

"Yes. Are you gonna teach him while Grandpa works with me?"

Her son's eagerness took hold of her, producing a smile. "I'm gonna try. That is, if he's a quick learner." She threw the man in question a glance and noticed him ambling over to them.

"What happens if I'm not a quick learner?" Joshua asked, ruffling Sean's hair.

"It might be kinda fun to see how you handle a runaway horse."

Sean giggled and turned his face up toward Joshua's. "Mom's just kidding. She has the patience of Job."

"I may be testing that, Sean," Joshua said, laughing.

"Are we all going to stand around jawing or are we gonna ride?"

"Grandpa, I'm ready." Sean hurried after his grandfather, who was heading into the barn.

Darcy exhaled a huge breath while she watched her son and father disappear inside.

Joshua took her hand and held it between his. "Sean and Shamus will be fine."

Darcy clenched her teeth, tension in every fiber of her being. "I'm not so sure." She tugged her hand free, putting space between them.

"Don't you know grandparents' relationships with their grandchildren are different from parents' with their children?"

A lump clogged her throat. She couldn't speak for fear her emotions would pour out.

"Besides, you're gonna have your hands full dealing with me. You've got to promise me before I get up on a horse that if it bolts you'll rescue me." Again he ran his thumb over and over his fingertips.

She moistened her throat. "But aren't you the rescuer?"

"A horse, madam, isn't a burning building."

Darcy started for the entrance. "I'm so glad you clarified that for me. For a moment I was confused."

His bark of laughter followed her into the barn. She found her father and Sean at the stall of a dark brown gelding—her son's horse. Her father finished putting the saddle on, showing Sean every step. Then her father led Sea Wave over to the mounting block and tightened the cinch on the saddle before allowing Sean to get on.

"Just remember, if Sean can do this, so can you."

"You certainly know how to motivate a guy."

"I use every means I can to get the job done." Darcy flipped her hand toward a stall at the other end of the barn. "That's your horse for today. Put her saddle on." She began walking away.

Joshua grabbed her arm. "Where do you think you're going?" Panic laced his question.

"To get my mare."

"I may not know much about riding, but I do know if you don't get your saddle on securely, you will fall off the horse."

"I know. But we learn so much better from our mistakes."

He covered the area between them. "You're enjoying this way too much."

First she smiled, then she laughed. "Yes."

Somehow he shrank the space between them, his breath fanning her cheek. "I'm glad. I don't like seeing you upset. Remember we're here to have fun. Now, show me how to put on the saddle."

"First you flatter, then you demand. You have an unique way of getting what you want."

"Is it working?"

Shaking her head, she stepped around him toward the stall where his horse was. She drew in several deep breaths to still the racing of her pulse. His nearness threatened her resolve to keep an emotional distance.

Darcy brought the gray mare out into the middle of the barn to demonstrate how to secure the saddle. She was aware of Joshua's close scrutiny and her hands actually quivered. When he took the strap to tighten the girth, their fingers brushed and an electrical current zipped up her arm. She quickly moved back several paces, feeling the strong beat of her heart against her chest.

"Mom, look at me."

At the sound of her son's voice she whirled about.

He was seated on Sea Wave, his posture correct, a wide grin on his face. He waved at her and she gave him a thumbs-up. While her father prepared his stallion to ride, Sean waited with the reins in his hands, watching everything his grandfather was doing.

Ten minutes later Darcy mounted her mare while Joshua surged into the saddle as though he had been doing it for years. He flashed her a grin. "I'm a quick study."

"And I get the impression not much scares you, really."

"After facing a wall of fire coming at me, you're probably right."

"What is it about men and doing risky things?"

"It's my job."

"That's what my husband used to say—and his job killed him."

"When it's my time to leave here, then it's my time. I can't let fear govern my life or I wouldn't be able to do my job."

"There's nothing wrong with a healthy dose of fear." Darcy jerked her reins to the left and set her mare into a trot.

"I agree." Joshua trailed after her, out into the sunshine. "It's what makes me pause and check out a situation before tackling it. I don't rush into a burning building without assessing it first."

"That's comforting to know." Darcy clamped her lips together before she said anything else that would give away her growing feelings for the man riding beside her.

"Watch out, Darcy O'Brien, you might actually start to care."

She shot him an exasperating look. "I care. You're a friend and I prefer that nothing happens to a friend."

"We can't live forever. What's important is what we do with our time on earth. I want no regrets when I die."

"So you don't have *any* regrets?" She pulled on the reins to halt her mare's progress, allowing her father and Sean to ride ahead.

Joshua brought his horse up next to hers. "I didn't say that. I have regrets. I'm just working on cutting them down, that's all."

"Your approach to life is a lot like my husband's was. And look what happened to him." Though their marriage hadn't been a good one, she'd lived in fear every time he'd gone up in his fighter jet. He'd loved the rush and thrill of defying the laws of nature.

"Did your husband believe in God?" Joshua shaded his eyes with his hand, his gaze intent.

"My husband believed only in himself," she said with all the bitterness that had built up in her over the years she'd been married.

"Then we aren't alike at all. I put my faith and my life in God's hands. That's not to say I don't believe in my-self. I've been trained well to do what I do. There's only a certain amount of our life we can control—for the rest we just have to have faith in the Lord that He knows best."

"I wish I could feel that way."

"Why can't you?"

"Because I'm not sure I know who I am." Darcy spurred her mare forward, needing to put an end to the conversation before she confessed the struggle she was going through to discover the woman left after Clay's sudden death. Coming home had put her personal journey into a nosedive.

She caught up to her father and son on the trail to the creek as they headed into a grove of trees. There the cool breeze died, replaced by the cool shade. The scent of damp earth and pine vied with leather and horse. Several birds sang above her, while the sound of water rushing over rocks resonated through the woods.

This was her favorite place on the farm. When she was a little girl, she came here to think...or to cry. She almost hated the idea of coming here now with her father because this had been where she'd come to escape the stress of trying to be perfect for him.

Her emotions warring, she stopped near the stream and dismounted. "This place hasn't changed," she murmured, making a slow circle, taking in the tranquility that surrounded her. Physically at least...but spiritually it had changed. She wasn't the same little girl who had fought every day for her father's approval. That much she knew about herself. Somewhere along the line she'd given up. Hadn't she?

"Beautiful." Joshua came up next to her.

Sunlight shot through the openings in the tree canopy to flood the forest floor as though gold poured from the heavens to mingle with the browns and greens of earth. A merging of two worlds. Darcy wanted to dance in the streams of light, lift her face up and let them bathe her in warmth.

"Yes, it is," she said.

A yellow butterfly, soaring on an air current, passed in front of her. She watched it disappear into the thick grove on the other side of the creek and wished she could follow.

"Did you see me, Joshua?" Sean ran up to him. "Grandpa says I'm a natural."

Darcy's gaze fastened onto her father, upstream, holding the reins of both horses. Weariness showed in the deepening lines about his mouth and eyes. "Dad, why don't we sit and rest here for a while?"

He came alert. "I don't need to rest."

"You might not, but I do. I haven't been here in years and would like to enjoy it for a while."

Tension seemed to siphon from him, sagging his shoulders. "Fine. I'd forgotten this was your favorite place."

"It was, Mom?" Sean asked.

Darcy nodded, her gaze still fixed on her father as he dropped the reins and eased down onto a large boulder near the creek. Seeing him wince brought words of caution to her mouth. She dug her teeth into her lower lip to keep them inside. Her father wouldn't appreciate them.

"Are there fish in this stream?" Sean peered into the clear, cool water.

"Yes, but I don't think there are any that you would want to eat. Most are too small."

Joshua stretched his muscles. "Do you like to fish, Sean?"

"I don't know. I haven't gone fishing before."

"Well, tell you what. I'll take you one day and we'll see. Sweetwater Lake is a great place to fish."

"Can Mom come, too?"

"Sure." Joshua flashed her a grin. "That is, if you want to. You're welcome to come too, Shamus."

Her father shook his head and waved his hand. "Never did like to sit still long enough to catch anything. Too impatient for fishing."

Sean's brow furrowed. "How long do you have to sit still? I don't know if I can, either."

Joshua's wide shoulders rose in a shrug. "That depends on how the fish are biting. The place I'll take you is a good fishing hole. Probably not too long."

"Good. My teacher says I squirm too much in my desk."

"I had that same problem, but I've managed to fish." Joshua eased down onto the grass-covered ground next to Darcy and leaned back against a large oak.

Sean picked up some pebbles and tried to skip them. They plunked into the water, the sound slicing through the silence.

"It's all in which pebbles you select, son." Her father motioned for Sean to come to him, and he began to instruct her son in how to skip rocks.

Darcy listened to her father's patient words and marveled at them. *Thank you, Lord, for that.*

"Your father's good with Sean." Joshua took a blade of grass and chewed on it.

"Yes." The word came out bitter sounding, and she immediately regretted her tone. Her own relationship with her father shouldn't color her son's.

"But he wasn't with you?"

"I can count on one hand the number of times he was patient with me when showing me something."

"Maybe he's changed. Mellowed out."

"Maybe," she said with all the cynicism she had developed over the years in regard to her father.

"Was that why you stayed away all these years?"

She clenched and unclenched her hands. "Yes. I only had so much emotional energy." *And I'd used it all up trying to keep my marriage together,* she added silently. "I know I shouldn't have stayed away. I won't again. I'm stronger now. I can deal with my father for a few weeks a year."

"That's good. Sean's connecting with his grandfather."

Darcy's gaze found her son standing next to her father, intent on what Shamus was saying. Sean picked up a pebble, examined it and tossed it back. Selecting another one, he tried it. The flat stone skipped two times across the stream.

"Way to go, Sean." Her father patted her son on the back. "You're gonna be a pro in no time."

"You think, Grandpa?"

"Sure."

Darcy turned away, her throat tight. Feeling vulnerable and guilty made each breath she took difficult. The constriction in her throat spread to encompass her chest. Sean's laughter echoed through the woods. With her eyes squeezed closed, she listened to the two men in her life and wished she felt connected.

Joshua laid his hand over hers. Her eyes snapped open and she looked into his.

"Ten years can make a difference, Darcy. Talk to your father. Let him know how you feel, especially about the past."

"How do you tell someone you love that you don't want to be around them?" Her question took even her by surprise.

"When I have a particularly difficult problem, I pray for guidance. You aren't alone. You have me. You have God—"

"Ready to head back?" Her father approached with his arm about Sean.

Darcy swallowed once, then twice before she thought she could answer. "Yes. There are still a lot of chores that need to be done."

"And a puppy to pick up," Sean said, snatching his reins.

"Here, I'll give you a leg up." Joshua pushed himself to his feet, a groan escaping his lips. "I don't think I should have sat down. That was a big mistake. My muscles are protesting."

"If you aren't used to riding, that certainly can happen." Darcy took her reins and grabbed hold of her saddle to hoist herself up.

Joshua rolled his eyes, his first few steps toward Sean rigid. "*Now* you tell me."

"You just have to work the stiffness out, Joshua." Her father mounted his stallion and waited.

Sean vaulted into his saddle with Joshua's help. "Can we go faster on the way back to the barn?"

"Sure, once we hit the meadow—" her father

paused and threw her a glance "—that is, if it's okay with your mom."

Shocked that he'd asked her opinion, Darcy nodded. While Sean and her father headed back through the woods toward the pasture, she watched Joshua pull himself into his saddle, a grimace on his face.

"Are you that sore?"

"Afraid so. I keep in shape, but obviously a whole different set of muscles is involved in riding." He stared after the disappearing pair. "Do me a favor?"

"What?"

"Let's take it slow and easy."

Darcy suppressed her laugh. "I can handle that."

But could she handle a man like Joshua? Each day she was around him she grew to like and care about him more and more. Against her nature she was finding herself confiding in him, which should be setting off alarm bells in her mind. But it felt so natural and right.... *We're just friends,* she thought—and was afraid she was lying to herself.

"Come in. Crystal has been so excited since you called." Tanya Bolton stepped to the side to allow Darcy and Sean into her house.

Sean cradled his new puppy to his chest. "At church Wednesday night Crystal told me she loved dogs. I wanted to show her my new one."

"She's back in the den. Why don't you take your puppy back there and show her?" Tanya pointed toward the hallway. "While he's doing that, would you like something to drink? I have sodas, iced tea, water?" She walked through the dining room into the kitchen.

"Water is fine." Darcy noticed the stack of dirty dishes in the sink and some pots with dried food in them left on the stove. Two houseplants on the windowsill over the sink were wilting and turning brown.

After pouring some iced water from a pitcher in the refrigerator, Tanya indicated a chair at her oak table in front of a large picture window that offered a view of the small backyard.

"Since the accident Crystal hasn't had too many of her friends over. We've been pretty tied up and haven't even had a chance to go to church until a few weeks ago."

"Sean said Crystal is in his summer Sunday school class that Joshua teaches for the upper elementary grades."

"She'll graduate to the next level next summer. She starts the sixth grade next fall—that is, if she goes to school."

Darcy lifted the glass to her lips, the cool liquid sliding down her dry throat. "Why wouldn't she?"

"Tom doesn't want her to go to school now that she's in a wheelchair." Tanya dropped her gaze to her hand that held the drink. "In fact, he isn't too happy that I'm taking her to church. He wants—" She looked at Darcy, tears in her eyes. "He thinks she's better off being home-schooled and staying here. I won't hide my daughter. I can't—" Tanya cleared her throat and took a large gulp of water. "I don't know what to do."

Darcy's heart ached for the woman sitting across from her. She reached out and covered Tanya's hand with hers. "All we can do is what we think is best. As long as I'm here, I'll help you any way I can."

Tanya choked back a sob. "Thanks. I feel so alone lately. I've lost touch with my friends. After the accident I spent every waking moment with Crystal. I'm trying to get my old life back together but—" she cleared her throat "—it's difficult sometimes, especially when I can't seem to stay on top of things that I know I should."

Darcy could relate to this woman. Making changes in one's life was never easy. "Remember, if you need help, I'm just a call away. Maybe Crystal can come visit the farm."

Horror flitted across Tanya's features. "No. Tom would get so angry if I brought her out to your farm. I'm not even going to say anything to him about your visit."

"Well, then, we can always bring Lady over to see Crystal again if she wants."

"We'll see—" They heard a noise coming from the front of the house, and Tanya jumped, fear widening her eyes. She shot to her feet and hurried from the kitchen, saying, "I'll be back in a sec."

"I'm sorry, Mrs. Bolton. Lady got away from us."

Darcy followed the sound of her son's voice and found him in the entry hall with Tanya. Crystal had wheeled herself down the hallway. A trash can lay on its side with crumpled papers scattered over the tile floor.

"Mom, Lady likes trash cans. Isn't that funny?" Crystal patted her lap and Sean put the puppy where she indicated. "Can we go outside? Sean says he's gonna teach her to fetch."

"Crystal, you know we haven't made the deck and backyard handicap accessible yet."

Crystal pouted. "But Dad promised he would last month."

"He'll get around to it. For the time being you'll have to be satisfied with the den. But no fetching in there."

As Sean walked behind Crystal toward the den, Tanya sighed, tears springing to her eyes again. "I hate disappointing her. But she needs several ramps built in order for her to go out back. And to tell you the truth, Tom's always working. He's rarely here anymore, so I don't know when they're going to be built."

"Maybe Joshua knows someone who can build them."

Tanya's eyes grew round. "Oh, no. Tom would be furious if anyone else did it. He wants to do everything himself. He'll get to it sometime."

When they were back in the kitchen, Tanya asked, "I understand from Reverend Collins that you're just visiting for the summer, that you live in Panama City. What do you do down there?"

Darcy told Tanya about her job and the purchase of her very first house not on a Navy base, while Tanya talked about her volunteer work before her daughter's accident. The mention of the accident brought tears to

Tanya's eyes and again Darcy comforted the woman, not sure how to help her. Tanya's emotions seemed so close to the surface.

Suddenly Tanya glanced at the clock over the stove and stood. "I hate to end this, but Tom will be home in an hour and I need to start dinner. Thank you so much for bringing Sean and his puppy by. Maybe he can visit another time."

Five minutes later Sean and Darcy were ushered from the house. Sean spun back to wave goodbye to Crystal, who had wheeled herself to the glass door. The forlorn look on the child's face tore at Darcy.

After the summer horse auction at the fairgrounds, Darcy decided, she would make it a point to get more involved with Crystal and Tanya. Crystal needed a friend, and Tanya needed…Darcy wasn't sure what, but the woman was close to falling apart. She intended to talk with Lizzy about Tanya Bolton. Maybe Lizzy had some suggestions to help her with the woman.

On the ride back to the farm Sean held Lady in his arms and stared out the side window. His silence was so unusual that Darcy asked, "What's wrong?"

"I'm thinking about Crystal. She doesn't leave the house much and she misses her friends. She wants a puppy like Lady."

"You know what might be nice for Crystal is a therapy dog. I'll do some research on them and say something to her mother."

"Mom, I'd like to visit again. When can I?"

"Let me see after the horse auction. My time is going

to be pretty filled with that coming up. We'll be auctioning off fifteen horses."

"Can I help?"

"Sure. The more we do, the less Grandpa will have to do. It's at the end of next week."

When Darcy pulled into the farm, she headed the truck toward one of the broodmare barns. "I've got to check on the new mare. Why don't you go on up to the house and tell Lizzy we're back so she'll start dinner?"

"I'm hungry. Maybe I can get a snack." Sean hopped from the truck and let Lady down.

As he started running toward the house, Darcy shouted, "Don't spoil your dinner. No cookies or sweets."

He turned and jogged backward, Lady at his heel. "Aw, Mom."

"You heard me, young man. You can have one piece of fruit."

"He reminds me of you when you were a child."

Darcy gasped, spinning around to face Jake.

"You had quite a sweet tooth if I remember correctly."

"I still do. How's the new mare adjusting to her new home?"

"Fine. She's out in the pasture right now." Jake walked toward the barn. "I put her up next to Butterfly at the end."

"Dad thinks she'll be a good breeder."

"Your father's rarely wrong."

When it came to horses that was true, but when it

came to people… She moved toward the back stall to check the mare, while Jake headed for the tack room. The scent of fresh hay gave her a feeling of having come home. She'd missed the horses and the farm—she hadn't realized how much.

"I like being a librarian," she muttered to herself, closing the door to the stall. "I like working with children."

"Should I be worried about you talking to yourself?"

Darcy peered toward the rafters, then slowly turned toward Joshua. "There are several mares within earshot."

"Oh. That makes all the difference."

She placed her hands on her waist and cocked her head. "Are you making fun of me?"

"I won't answer that. Not if I want you to do me a favor."

"What?"

"I need a date for next Thursday night."

A date? Oh, my! All her alarm bells sounded.

Chapter Six

"Yes, a date." Joshua grinned, his blue eyes glinting. "With all that has been going on I forgot about the awards dinner."

"What awards dinner?" Darcy asked.

Joshua actually turned a nice shade of red. "I'm being given an award for rescuing a woman and child from a burning house."

"What an honor!"

The blush deepened. He looked away, his thumb rubbing across his fingers. "I shouldn't have gone into the house, but I couldn't let the woman and her toddler die. I was lucky. I got them and myself out without anyone being too seriously injured. My captain was not happy about the risk I took, but the governor is giving me an award."

There was that word again—*risk*. Darcy was beginning to hate it.

"God was looking out for me that night."

"Well, I'm glad someone was." Her mouth set in a taut line, she started for the entrance.

Joshua fell into step next to her. "Why are you upset? Everything worked out okay."

"I'm not upset," she said, then realized that wasn't the truth. "One day it might not work out. Have you ever really stopped and thought about that?"

Clasping her arm in the middle of the yard, he stopped and turned her to face him. "What would you have me do? Stand by and do nothing while someone was trapped in a burning building? I had to try and get them out."

Her anger deflated. "No." Her gaze dropped to the ground. "I would have tried, too."

He placed his finger under her chin and lifted her head. His gaze locked with hers. "You did do the same thing when your barn was burning. You went in to get the horses out because you couldn't stand by and watch them burn."

She closed her eyes for a few seconds, the image of the frightened horses imprinted on her mind. When she stared into his eyes again, she felt lost in the vivid blue of his gaze. Time fell away, leaving only them.

She didn't want to care about Joshua Markham, but she did.

"Yes, I'll go. What time will you pick me up?"

"Six. We have to drive to Lexington."

"How should I dress?"

"I have to wear a suit."

"You make it sound like a sentence."

"I don't particularly like to wear a suit and tie."

"Then I guess I won't wear my jeans and boots."

His chuckle danced up her spine. "In horse country that wouldn't be too far-fetched, but since the governor and other dignitaries are going to be there, you'd better don a dress."

"The governor? This must have been a big deal."

Joshua plowed his fingers through his hair and peered over her shoulder with a wry grin on his face. "The woman I rescued was a niece of the governor's."

"So you have friends in high places."

"The only one that counts is God."

Darcy started again for the main house. She wished she had his strong faith. But doubts plagued her.

"Dinner's gonna be ready shortly. Do you want to stay?"

"Sure. Why else do you think I waited until this time to ask?"

She glanced at him, his face full of laughter. "You know, underneath it all, I think you're serious."

"For a man who hates to cook and isn't very good when he has to, you're probably right."

"So I should expect you to appear on my doorstep around seven whenever you aren't working?"

"Is that an invitation?"

The eagerness in his voice produced a laugh from Darcy. "I shouldn't encourage you."

"But I'm so adorable when I'm begging."

She shook her head and entered the house through the kitchen. Lizzy glanced up from stirring something on the stove.

"Dinner is in fifteen minutes."

"I've invited Joshua to join us again. Can I help you with anything?"

"You can get another place setting down for him. Joshua, Shamus and Sean are in the den. Will you tell them dinner is almost ready?" After Joshua left, Lizzy added, "You can also get the salad out of the refrigerator."

Darcy took a deep breath, delicious aromas enticing her. "What are we having?"

"Chicken stew. Nothing fancy, but something on your father's diet."

Darcy removed the salad from the refrigerator along with some bottles of dressing, all low fat, she noticed. "Now that Joshua's gone, what did you want to talk to me about?"

Lizzy wiped her hands on a towel tucked into the waistband of her apron. "Tanya Bolton. We've known each other too long to beat around the bush on anything. Be careful, child. Tanya is dealing with a lot of issues."

Reaching for another plate, Darcy stopped and dropped her arm to her side, spinning about to look at Lizzy. "I know she has a lot of issues. Her husband for one, her daughter's accident for another. What are you not telling me?"

Lizzy sighed heavily, leaning back against the counter and folding her arms across her chest. "Tanya is bipolar."

The room seemed to tilt for a few seconds. Darcy gripped the edge of the counter and steadied herself.

"She's been on medication for several years and was doing fine until her daughter's accident. Everything has turned upside down for Tanya. I've tried to help when I can, but her husband denies there's a problem with his wife and prefers the family not be involved with the community."

"Not a nice man if you ask me, and I haven't even met him."

"Tom has had a difficult road. A lot has happened to him in the past few years. He was doing all right until Crystal got hurt. He used to come to church regularly. He used to be involved in the community. Now he stays to himself."

"Crystal needs to be around friends. He doesn't even want her and Tanya to come to church."

"Sound like someone we know?"

"Dad." The name was wrenched from Darcy's soul, bringing back all kinds of memories of what happened after her mother died. She had so needed her father to help her to understand her loss. Her legs weakened, and Darcy slid to the floor, burying her face in her hands.

The housekeeper squatted next to her. "Now you know why I needed to warn you to be careful. Maybe you shouldn't help Tanya."

Tears stung Darcy's eyes. Memories continued to flood her. She was a teenager again, desperately trying to figure out why her mother had killed herself, needing her father's comfort. Instead, she'd received anger and coldness. He had rejected the Lord and turned away from the church, just like Tom. Tanya and her situation weren't the same, but there was a connection. Her mother had suffered from manic depression too.

"But she's so alone, Lizzy."

"You're going to be gone in a few months. Do you really want to get involved in something like that? I was hoping I wouldn't have to tell you about Tanya because I knew how it would affect you." Lizzy hugged her as she had when Darcy had been trying to make sense of her mother's death.

"I couldn't help my mother, but maybe I can help Tanya now that I know what she's going through." Tears coursed down her cheeks. "I've got to try."

"I figured you would say that. It isn't your battle, and you have more than enough to handle with your father right now."

Darcy shoved herself to her feet. "I can always count on you to look out for me." *Is God giving me a second chance through Tanya to understand what drove my mother to kill herself? Would understanding Tanya's situation help me to understand my father?* Questions bombarded her that she had no answers to.

"Child, I'm here if you need to talk."

"I know." Darcy turned back to the cabinet and retrieved a plate and glass for Joshua. "I've always been able to count on you."

"But not your father?"

"Do I have to answer that question?" Darcy opened the drawer and selected a fork, spoon and knife.

"No. Your father can be one of the stubbornest men I've known."

"And you still work for him."

"Someone's got to watch out for him. He certainly isn't doing a very good job of it."

Seeing the slight coloring in Lizzy's cheeks made Darcy think back over the past few weeks to when the housekeeper and her father were together. Lizzy could get away with saying things to him that no one else could. He argued with her, but he also listened to what she had to say. Was there more going on between them? Lizzy had put up with him for as many years as her mother had.

"Joshua has been spending a lot of time with you and Sean. Is there something you would like to tell me?"

"Are you trying to change the subject?"

"Yes, is it working?"

Darcy laughed. "Joshua and I are friends. He's wonderful with Sean, and Sean likes to be around him."

"Just Sean." Lizzy sent her a sharp, appraising look.

"Okay, I like to be around him, too, but as you just pointed out to me, I'll be leaving in less than two months, so nothing is going to happen beyond friendship."

"If you say so." Lizzy reached for the serving bowl and a spoon. "Please set the table."

Darcy went into the dining room and arranged a place setting for Joshua, then headed for the den to see what was keeping the guys. When she entered, she heard her father and Joshua talking about the fires. Stopping at the entrance, she searched the room for her son. He wasn't there.

"All four of the fires are connected, sir. So far no one's been injured, but several horses died and a great deal of property has been destroyed."

"If I get my hands on the person responsible for doing this, he'll regret the day he was born."

"That's not looking very promising right now, unless we catch him red-handed. Arson cases can be difficult to solve, and when there's no obvious reason, it's even harder. Sometimes we find the arsonist likes to watch the fire he sets, but in this case, because of the isolation of the barns, that isn't happening. At least, where we can see him. The only crowds gathering are the people who live on the farms who are trying to rescue the horses and help put the fire out."

"What if he's hiding?"

"That's possible. Everyone's busy with the fire, so it would be hard to tell." Joshua exhaled a deep breath. "At least everyone in the area has hired additional guards to protect their barns and horses. I think that's one reason we haven't seen another fire in several weeks since the Colemans'. Maybe there won't be any more."

Her father shifted in his overstuffed chair, caught sight of her and waved her into the room. "Did you take a look at Angus Feehan? I heard he was fired from another stable a few weeks back. Pretty hotheaded man when riled."

"Riled enough to burn barns?"

Her father rubbed his chin and thought for a moment.

"The more I think about him, the more it seems a strong possibility."

"We have checked him out. He doesn't have good alibis for the fires. He lives by himself and says he was home sleeping. No one to say one way or the other."

"You'd better keep an eye on him. He's got shifty eyes if you ask me."

Joshua chuckled. "The police can't arrest everyone who has shifty eyes."

"I know, but I never trusted him or Mike Reynolds. Both have reason to burn my barn."

"But the others?"

"I know Mike worked for the Andersons before coming to work for me. So he's worked for three of the four farms hit. A mighty big coincidence."

"Dad, where's Sean? Dinner is ready."

Her father labored to stand. When he saw Darcy frowning at him, he said, "I probably should get another chair to sit in. That one is getting harder and harder for an old man to get out of."

"That's the first time I've heard you refer to yourself as old."

Her father's gaze pinned her. "How would you know? You haven't been around much in the past ten years to know what I say or think."

Darcy felt as though her father had slapped her in the face. She automatically took a step back, her hand coming up to her throat.

He stalked past her, muttering, "Sean took Lady outside to…go. I'll get him."

"Sean named his dog Lady?"

Joshua's question reminded her that she wasn't alone and that she needed to regain her composure quickly or she would find herself breaking down in front of him.

"Yes." She averted her head as though she were watching her father leave, when in actuality she didn't see much through the sheen of tears.

"That was what I called my first dog."

She blinked the tears away before facing Joshua. "I know. Sean didn't think a girl dog should be called Joshua, but he liked the name Lady so he calls her that because of you."

Joshua approached her, his gaze connected to hers. "I'm sorry, Darcy."

"About what?" Her throat thickened again, and she felt the walls of the den close in on her.

Joshua gestured toward where her father had disappeared. "What I just witnessed between you and your father."

She attempted a smile that wavered about the corners of her mouth and faltered. "It's not a secret our relationship is rocky at best."

"And the added tension with the fires makes everyone on edge."

"Don't make excuses for him. The fires have nothing to do with it."

"Then what does?"

Aware of the compassion she saw in the blue depths of his eyes, she wanted to tell him everything—starting with her mother's illness and suicide. The words wouldn't come out. Instead she pressed her lips together and pivoted, heading for the dining room before she did confide in him.

What good would it do? Her mother would still be dead. Her relationship with her father would still be awful. And Joshua would own a part of her that she didn't share with others. Even Lizzy, who had been around, didn't know the depths of her agony over finding her mother and the suicide note.

Darcy ran her hand over her ice-green silk dress for probably the hundredth time since leaving the farm for Lexington. Her nerves were strung so tight she was afraid they would snap. A date! She hadn't been on one in years and wasn't sure what to do. She hoped it was like riding a bicycle because she was working herself up into a frenzy over it.

She glanced at Joshua, his large, strong hands on the steering wheel, his gaze trained forward on the highway, and wondered why she had accepted this date. It was a complication she didn't need.

But a welcome distraction, a tiny voice inside her said. The past few days at the farm had been hectic with getting ready for the horse auction. The bite of her father's words still stung from earlier today: she hadn't had all the paperwork done the way he had wished. No matter that she had never done it before and was learning—

"No frowns allowed tonight," Joshua said.

"Sorry about that. Just thinking of all the preparation that goes into selling the horses."

"That's this weekend, isn't it?"

"Yes. Dad's beside himself. He's angry that he doesn't feel one hundred percent yet, so he has to rely on me to do some of the things he's always done."

"He's a proud man. His illness has been difficult on him."

"Why is it so hard for some people to accept help?"

He flashed her grin. "Beats me. I accept all kinds of help. For instance, I need an assistant to help me with my Sunday school class for the rest of the summer. Marge had a family emergency and will be gone quite a bit." He waggled his brows. "Any takers in this truck?"

Darcy twisted around, checking the cab out. "I don't see any." She paused, then added, "Unless you're referring to me."

"How about it?"

"I won't be able to this weekend. I'll be so involved with the horse auction that I'm sure I'll meet myself coming and going."

"You can start the next Sunday, then. I'm not picky."

"Gee, I'm not sure I shouldn't be offended."

"Will it make things better if I tell you that you were the first and only person I thought to ask?"

"Now, flattery works much better."

"I aim to please." Joshua pulled into the hotel parking garage and found a place immediately on the ground level. "A good sign. This will be a nice evening."

"Of course it will, I'm your date." As they left the garage, she linked her arm through his, her spirits lifted at the prospects of spending an evening with Joshua.

She wouldn't think about the farm for the next few hours. Tomorrow would be here soon enough and all the problems she'd left behind would still be there.

Darcy marveled at the beautifully decorated ballroom of the hotel. It was a study in gold and glittering crystal. Elegant. Richly ornate. "You didn't tell me half the population of Kentucky was going to be here."

"This is an annual event. The governor honors certain people who have done extraordinary things, from research scientists at the university to police officers."

"To you."

He leaned close to her ear, his breath tickling her neck. "I think you're trying to get me to blush again."

They were escorted to a table at the front of the room and seated with a police officer from Lexington and his wife, a businesswoman who financed a relief program for a small town that had suffered from a devastating tornado, and a minister and his wife who ran a program for the needy in eastern Kentucky. Darcy felt honored to be among such people.

Listening to them talk put some of Darcy's problems in perspective. Even though she was only going to be in Sweetwater for a while longer, there wasn't any reason not to become involved in the community. And she knew where she wanted to start—with Tanya and Crystal Bolton. Tanya needed help and a friend. She could do both.

By the time the awards dinner was over, Darcy had a plan. She and Joshua, plaque in hand, left the hotel after being bombarded by the press and people who wanted to congratulate Joshua for his rescue. Noticing that he blushed and continually ran his thumb over his fingers, she smiled to herself. He wasn't comfortable with all this attention, but she was glad she had come. She had seen another side of Joshua. Usually he was so self-assured, but up at the podium he was out of his element. He'd said a few words of thanks but had sat down almost immediately, having given the shortest speech of the evening.

"If I hadn't seen it with my own two eyes, I wouldn't have believed you were shy, Joshua Markham."

"I don't like crowds and I certainly don't like to give a speech in front of strangers. If you hadn't agreed to come, I'm not sure I would have shown up."

She stopped, facing him. "Not come? You're kidding! The governor was giving you a plaque honoring your heroism and you weren't going to come?"

He shrugged and reached around her to open the passenger door of his truck. "What can I say? I was a nervous wreck all day. The guys at the station were ready to demand I go home early from work."

"Going into a burning building doesn't scare you, but getting up in front of a crowd of strangers does?"

"Yep. That about sums it up."

Darcy shook her head. "I don't understand you. You get up in church and with the kids in your Sunday school class."

"That's different. I know those people and it's never about me."

"Ah, I see. So if the church gave you an award for your work you wouldn't be embarrassed?"

He nodded. "I don't do these things to call attention to myself or for any kind of reward."

"Why do you do them?"

"Because God gave me a gift and I'm using it the way He wants me to. Someone's gotta fight fires and work with the kids at church."

Darcy climbed into the cab of the truck and waited until Joshua rounded the front and slipped behind the steering wheel before saying, "I have a favor to ask."

He started the engine. "What?"

"I want to build some ramps for Crystal in her backyard so she can enjoy going outside, and I need help to do that."

"I'd love to. Have you asked Tanya and Tom?"

"Well, no, not yet, but Tanya mentioned she needed some ramps built. Do you think Tom will mind if I offer?"

"Honestly, I don't know. I haven't seen him in months, and the stories I've heard lead me to believe he might."

"That's what Tanya thought. She said something about Tom wanting to build them himself but never getting around to it. I guess all I can do is ask. Maybe he'll surprise us all and agree."

Darcy settled in the seat and leaned her head back. Joshua switched on some soft, classical music, and the peaceful strains tempted her to close her eyes—just for a few minutes, she thought. The next thing she knew,

Joshua was shaking her awake, his deep voice whispering to her.

She bolted upright, noticing he was driving down the lane that led to her house. "I didn't mean to fall asleep. You should have said something. I've been functioning for the past week on about half the sleep I require. I guess it finally caught up with me."

He breathed a deep sigh of relief. "Good. For a while there I thought it might be a statement about my scintillating conversation."

The teasing tone in his voice relaxed her. "You can drop me off at the far barn."

"Surely you aren't going to work tonight?"

"I need to check on a mare. I promised Dad I would when I came home. It was either that or *he* would have, and he was exhausted."

"And you aren't?"

"I just had an hour nap. I'm refreshed and ready to go. Besides, it should only take a minute to make sure she didn't go into labor."

"Then I'll wait for you and drive you up to the house."

"You don't have to do that."

"Yes, I do." As he stopped the truck in front of the barn, his gaze met hers.

In the yard light she saw the gleam in his eyes and the look of determination in his expression. He wouldn't take no for an answer. "Okay. I won't be long."

She slid from the cab, and as he started to open his door, she said, "Stay. You won't even know I'm gone." And she hurried toward the barn.

Inside she made her way toward the second-to-last stall as quickly as possible in three-inch high heels. After checking on the mare, who was doing fine, she closed the door and started back toward the entrance. A noise to the left of her caught her attention. She halted, suddenly wondering where the guard was. Scanning the barn, she realized she was the only other person here. The noise was probably the cat in the tack room, she thought and resumed walking.

A *crash* had her spinning around and rushing toward the tack room, heedless of the danger she might be in. Approaching the door, she lifted her arm to push it open. Suddenly it banged open and she came face to face with a short man in dirty clothes and a shaggy beard that obscured his features. But the pale blue of his eyes imprinted itself on her brain. She screamed.

He shoved past her, sending her flying back. She hit the hard-packed dirt with a *thud*. She was scrambling to her feet when she heard Joshua running toward her.

"Are you all right? What happened?"

She waved her hand toward the rear of the barn. "He went that way."

Without another word Joshua sprinted toward the back and disappeared from view. Darcy pushed herself to her feet, vaguely aware that her beautiful new silk dress was probably ruined. She kicked off her high heels, then headed after Joshua. She ran into him—literally—just outside the barn.

"Did you see the man?"

"No, he was gone. Did you know him?"

"No, he was a stranger."

"Where's your father's guard?"

"Probably making his rounds—at least, I hope so. What if something's happened to the man? What if that was the arsonist and—" She shuddered; she didn't like the direction her thoughts were taking.

Joshua drew her into his embrace. "Let's check the barn and make sure the man didn't leave anything behind. Then let's go find the guard."

"You mean that man might have rigged the barn to burn?"

Joshua gripped her hand. "Yes. On second thought, I want you to go around to my truck and wait until I check everything out."

"No."

Chapter Seven

"What do you mean, no?" Anger lines carved into Joshua's face.

"I mean, no I won't go and quietly wait for you to inspect the barn for something that might cause a fire."

He thrust his face within inches of hers. "What if a fire starts while I'm in the barn?"

"Then I'll be there to help get the horses out. Every second will count if a fire starts." She tugged her hand from his and put both of hers on her waist. "And let me make it perfectly clear, I will try to save any horses I can."

"And you call *me* a risk taker. What kind of behavior is that?" He spoke in a very controlled voice while he was stalking toward the rear door of the barn.

Darcy watched him for a few seconds before she hurried after him. "What are we looking for?"

His look conveyed his displeasure at her insistence on being in the barn. "Anything unusual." He paused at the tack room door. "He was in here?"

"Yes."

"You check the stalls while I go through this room and the storage next door."

Five minutes into the inspection the guard showed up. Darcy sent him to check the other barn with any groom still on duty. She had visions of both barns going up at the same time.

Half an hour later Darcy stood with Joshua next to his truck, staring at the barn. "I'm glad we didn't find anything. But then, who was that man and why was he in there?"

Raking his fingers through his hair—not for the first time if its disheveled look meant anything—Joshua said, "We need to get a description to the police. He could be the arsonist. Even though we didn't find anything, maybe you came before he could set the fire."

"I guess I can't postpone talking to my father any longer. I told the guard not to say anything, that I would tell Dad. But before I do, I need to check with the guard to make sure the other barn is okay. If I can tell Dad everything's all right, he might take it better." Who was she kidding? Her father wouldn't take this well at all, but getting stressed over it would only make the situation worse.

"I'll drive you."

By the time Joshua parked in front of the main house, Darcy's shoulders sagged from exhaustion. What had started out as a delightful, fun-filled evening had evolved into a tension-filled nightmare, and she still had to face the worse part of it—her father.

Though it was after midnight, as she had suspected

her father was still up in the den, reading a horse magazine. His whole life revolved around his horses and the farm. What would happen to him if the farm was destroyed by an arsonist?

"Did you two have a good time?" Shamus looked up from his magazine as Darcy and Joshua entered.

"The food was good. The people we met were interesting."

"I hear a 'but' in your voice, son."

Joshua blew out a long breath. "I could have done with a little less pomp and circumstances."

"He hates to give speeches, but he did a great job. It was short and to the point." Darcy sat across from her father while Joshua stood next to her, his hand on her shoulder giving her silent support.

"I've got the feeling you want to tell me something."

"Dad, I checked on Dragonfly and she's doing fine." Her throat parched, Darcy tried to coat it but failed. Her mouth felt stuffed with cotton. "As I was leaving, I heard something in the tack room. When I went to investigate, a man rushed out and ran me down."

Her father surged to his feet and started for the door.

"Dad, wait!"

He pivoted, anger darkening his features, his deep gray eyes boring into her. His jaws clenched, he spoke through gritted teeth. "Where is he?"

"Gone, sir. I ran after him, but he disappeared."

"Did you know him?" Shamus asked Joshua.

"I didn't get a look at him. I was outside by my truck when I heard Darcy scream."

Her father shifted his attention to her. "Did you know him?"

She shook her head.

"What did he look like?"

"Short, dirty with a shaggy beard. His hair was dark and his eyes were a pale blue."

"Angus Feehan. That's got to be him. The last time I saw him he was growing a beard." Her father walked to the phone, put his hand on the receiver. "Did you check the barn?"

"Yes, sir. There was nothing. The guard and the groom on duty at night inspected the other one just to make sure. They even checked the new barn under construction."

Some of the tension seemed to leave Shamus as he picked up the receiver and placed a call to the police. While her father talked to the authorities, Joshua's hand on her shoulder squeezed gently, his gaze locking with hers as they walked from the room.

"I'd better go. I'm on duty tomorrow."

"Are you going to be able to come to the fairgrounds this weekend for any of the festivities?" Darcy asked when they were out in the entry hall.

"On Saturday. I'll stop by and see you. Tomorrow I'll talk with the police about Angus and see if he has a connection to the recent fires."

"It sure would be nice to find the person before anything else happens."

"Good night, Darcy." He leaned forward and kissed her on the cheek.

As he exited, her hand came up to touch the place where his lips had been only a few seconds before. The casual gesture left her weak and shaken. It was the kind of kiss that might transpire between two friends, and yet...

It felt so good to sit for a few minutes, Darcy thought as she eased into a lawn chair under the maple tree. Shade stretched out in a large circle offering a reprieve from the heat of a late June afternoon. People milled around, looking at the horses up for sale. The crowd's murmurs vied with the sounds coming from the fairway. The aroma of popcorn and grilled meat spiced the air, chasing away the scents of horses, sweat and hay.

Her father made his way toward her, taking the empty lawn chair nearby. He moaned as he sat. "I'm sure glad this will be over soon. We've done well." He stretched his long legs out in front of him and crossed them at the ankles. "I appreciate all your work, Darcy."

For a few seconds it seemed as if her heart had stopped beating. Maybe she hadn't heard her father correctly.

He reached over and patted her arm. "You did good."

A rush of emotions swamped her, robbing her of anything like a coherent reply. She fixed her gaze on a little boy running his hand over a mare's coat, a huge grin on his face.

"Child, did you hear me?"

"Yes," she finally replied, her voice heavy and full of those emotions she was trying to get under control.

Here in a crowd of people, her father was telling her she'd done a good job. A rare occurrence. "Thanks. I think the sales have gone well."

"One of the best years we've had, in spite of losing the barn a few weeks ago."

We? Not *I?* Again his statement produced a tightness in her throat that cut off the flow of words.

"I think we make a good team."

"Dad, are you all right?" *That's it. He's ill and trying to break the news gently.*

"Except for probably overdoing it today and yesterday, I'm fine. I'm nearly one hundred percent. Give me a few more weeks and there will be no stopping me." He twisted in the chair so he was looking at her. "Can't a person express their gratitude without you thinking there's something wrong?"

"Not when it's out of character."

"I realize I don't tell you how much I appreciate your efforts, but I do."

"Why now?"

"Why not?"

"That's not an answer, Dad."

"Okay, if you must know, Lizzy pointed out to me all you've been doing and that I haven't said anything to you. I realize you have given up your summer vacation to work on the farm, putting in twelve-hour days."

Ah, Lizzy. That explained everything. Disappointment surged within her. Someone had to tell him he should appreciate her efforts. Why couldn't he see that on his own?

"That's not to say I haven't seen all that you've been doing. I have. You know, girl, I'm not very good with words."

An understatement. "I'll stay this summer as long as you need me."

"Things should calm down some until fall, now that the big horse sale is over. I'll be able to work with Sean some more on riding. By the way, where is he?"

"He went with Nate to go on some of the rides. He has enough money for five of them, so he shouldn't be gone too long."

"Heard back from the police. They are charging Angus with trespassing but that's all. There isn't enough evidence for an arson charge."

"Maybe he didn't set the fires."

"Do you really believe he came back to the barn to retrieve some tack he left behind—what, three months ago?" Her father snorted. "He's lying."

"Dad, a groom found the tack he was talking about. He might not be lying."

"Oh, don't worry. I'm keeping the extra guard until this is resolved. In fact, I'm hiring another one. We have too many barns for just one. That became obvious with Angus's little escapade." He snorted again. "Tell me, child, if he'd left tack and was so concerned about it, why didn't he just come and get it during the day?"

"From what I understand, he didn't leave the farm under the best of circumstances. Didn't you physically throw him out?"

"He was smoking in the barn! What would you have

me do?" Her father rose, scanning the area. "I see some buyers over there. I'm gonna have a word with them."

He stalked off toward a group of four men near the second barn at the fairgrounds. Tact had never been her father's strong suit, Darcy thought, realizing she might have sneaked back in the dead of night for something she'd left behind, too.

"Haven't you heard frowning causes wrinkles?"

Joshua's question startled her, but she recovered quickly. "So does smiling and the sun."

He sat where her father had been only a moment before. "You know, I could stay right here and not move and probably enjoy what I like the most about the county fair."

"What?"

"People watching. People fascinate me. Like your father over there with those men. He knows them well. Even though they aren't from around here, he must see them every year at this horse auction."

"How do you know that?"

"Your father isn't a man who pats very many people on the back, but he greeted the taller man that way. That's familiarity, and because it is unusual for your father, the relationship must be one that's developed over many years."

"Maybe they live around here."

"No. I know most of the horse people in the area. Besides, when their car pulled up, the license plate was from Tennessee."

She playfully slapped him on the arm. "You're cheating."

"I never claimed I was Sherlock Holmes."

"Dad told me the police let Angus go."

"Yep. Nothing to keep him on." Joshua settled back in the lawn chair, stretching his legs out in front of him, just as her father had.

"You want to hear something funny? I found myself sticking up for Angus with my dad. Frankly, I don't know why. Angus could very well be the arsonist."

"Darcy, isn't it obvious? You and your dad butt heads. If your father said it was sunny out, I think you would argue it was cloudy."

Darcy straightened, glaring at Joshua. "I do not. I must admit we often don't see eye to eye, but—" She couldn't finish her sentence because she realized Joshua was probably right. When she lived here and when she was married to Clay, she'd kept her opinions to herself. Lately, though, she was learning to speak her mind, which often meant she and her father didn't agree.

"I didn't used to be that way. I used to bite my tongue, literally, rather than say anything that might rock the boat."

His gaze snared hers. "So now you're standing up for yourself?"

"Yes, but it hasn't been easy and I still have a long way to go. I know I need to choose the battles I fight with my father and sometimes I don't choose wisely. I'm learning."

"That's what life is all about."

Darcy lifted her hair from her neck, letting the cool breeze caress her skin. "I suppose you've never had that kind of problem."

"Nope, but I've had more than my share of other problems."

"Hi."

Approaching them at a fast pace were Crystal and Tanya. The older woman brought the wheelchair to a halt in front of Darcy. "Crystal wanted to see the horses, so I had to wait until Tom was busy judging the pies."

Darcy stood. "I'll go get one of the yearlings we have for sale."

"I'm so glad you suggested we stop by," Tanya said in a rush, moving around as though she couldn't keep her body still.

Darcy hurried into the barn and took the nearest horse from its stall, then led her to Crystal. The young girl leaned forward and touched the yearling, her face lit with a smile.

"I've missed riding."

Tanya put a hand on her daughter's shoulder. "She doesn't blame horses for what happened to her. I have to sneak in books about horses because her father would throw them away if he found them."

Darcy blinked, trying to keep up with Tanya's rapid fire speech. "If Crystal ever wants to ride again, I would be glad to arrange something."

Crystal dropped her hand away from the animal, shaking her head. "No, that's not possible. I can't walk."

"It's possible if you want to. People with your kind of injuries do ride."

Crystal thought for a moment, then shook her head again. "Dad would never let me."

Tanya scanned the area, her gaze darting from one thing to the next, never still for any length of time. "Speaking of your father, we'd better head back to the pavilion." She whirled the wheelchair about and started toward the fairway.

Darcy took the yearling back into the barn, then returned. "You know, I've never met Tom, but—" She looked toward the area where Joshua was staring. A small man, no more than five and a half feet tall, blocked Tanya's progress.

"That's Tom."

"Oh, no. He doesn't appear to be too happy."

"Definitely an understatement. Maybe I should go over there."

Before Joshua could move, Tom took the wheelchair from Tanya and began to push his daughter toward the parking lot. Tanya followed the pair. Darcy shivered, even though the air was warm.

"Has Reverend Collins spoken with Tom?" Darcy asked. She wanted to do something to help the family that was struggling with the fallout of such a tragic accident.

"Several times, but Tom made it clear he didn't want the reverend's help."

"He hasn't gotten past the anger stage of his grief."

"Some people never do. Some people need help in dealing with their grief, but won't accept it."

Could that apply to her father? After her mother's death, all she'd seen from her father was anger. Had he moved on? She didn't know because she hadn't been around for the past ten years.

"Can you steal away for a while and get an ice cream with me?" Joshua asked, coming to stand next to her.

His presence lifted her spirits. "I've never been able to turn down ice cream. Maybe we'll see Sean on the fairway. Let me tell Dad I'm going with you for a little while."

Darcy walked toward her father, who was shaking hands with each of the four men as they were leaving. His weathered face brightened with a smile.

"They're definitely interested in two of our jumpers. I'm sure they'll be bidding on them at the evening session."

"Dad, I'm going with Joshua for an ice cream. Can I get you anything from the fairway?"

"Nope." He rubbed the back of his neck. "You've been seeing a lot of Joshua lately. Is there anything going on that I should know about?"

There was actually a twinkle in her father's dark gray eyes that surprised Darcy. She almost forgot her father's question.

"Is there?"

Blinking, she finally replied, "Joshua and I are just friends. I'm helping him out at church with the Sunday school class."

"Is that what a few nights ago was? Funny, I would have thought you two had gone on a date. In my day that was what we called it."

Darcy lifted her shoulders in a shrug that she knew didn't convey the nonchalance she wanted to project. "That was different. He needed someone to go to the awards dinner with him."

"He couldn't go alone? I'm sure he wouldn't be the first or the last to do that."

She turned away. "I'll see you later." Her father's chuckles followed her all the way back to Joshua.

"You're blushing. What happened?"

"Nothing. Dad was just teasing me."

"Teasing you? From what I've gathered from you, that doesn't happen very often."

"If you must know, he thinks we're an item."

"And you set him straight," Joshua said, taking her by the elbow and steering her toward the fairway.

"Of course. We're just friends." And if she said it often enough, maybe she would believe it.

When had she begun to think of Joshua as more than a friend? The other evening at the awards dinner—their first official date? When he had chased Angus? When he had given her a peck on the cheek that curled her toes?

Before she knew it, she was standing in front of the ice cream truck and Joshua was asking her what flavor she wanted. She had been so lost in thoughts of Joshua that she hadn't even realized how she'd gotten there. Boy, she had it bad!

"Hmm. I like so many. I could have a triple scoop with each layer a different flavor."

"Talk about me taking risks. Do you know what that will do to your arteries?"

"Not to mention hips. Okay, I'll settle for a double-scoop butter pecan and cookie dough ice cream." Darcy's mouth watered as she waited for the woman behind the counter to make her cone. When the lady handed it to her, Darcy took a big lick and said, "Mmm, this is delicious. Isn't life grand?"

Sean and his friend Nate ran up to them. "I'd like an ice cream cone, too."

"How about the money you were given? Where is it?" Darcy asked, knowing perfectly well it had left his hands the minute he'd gotten it.

"Gone." He gave her an innocent look, meant to appeal to her good nature.

Which wasn't too hard with Joshua next to her and a beautiful day surrounding her. She dug into the pocket of her jeans. "Okay. But you'll need to check with Ken and see if there's anything he wants you to do. Nate, do you want one, too?"

"Yes, and I can help Sean with any chore he needs to do. Mom said she'd pick me up at the barn in an hour."

"Is your mother at the pavilion showing her dolls?" Darcy remembered being the recipient of Jesse's first doll-making attempt. She still had the doll displayed in her bedroom, which had annoyed Clay.

"Yes, ma'am."

After Darcy purchased the two ice-cream cones, the boys thanked her and took off toward the barns on the edge of the fairgrounds. She caught Joshua staring at her.

"You're a good mother, Darcy O'Brien. You have a solid relationship with your son."

Heat flooded her cheeks. "A lot of the time it was just

him and me. With Clay being gone so much, Sean and I became very close. I hate, though, that he doesn't have a man's influence in his life. I think that's important."

"He's taken to your father."

And you, Darcy thought. But both relationships were fleeting and hundreds of miles from their home in Panama City.

"Have you ever thought of having children? I've seen you with the kids at church and you're great with them."

His eyes conveyed a haunted look that struck a chord in Darcy. Remembering his ex-fiancée, she stepped closer, suddenly wanting to comfort him. "I'm sorry. I forgot about Carol."

"We'd talked about having children. I wanted at least three. She wasn't so sure she wanted any."

"And yet, she has a son now."

"I know I need to get past her betrayal, but we had known each other for years and I never saw it coming. It makes you doubt your judgment when something like that happens. It makes this risk taker—" he patted his chest "—cautious."

Someone jostled her, sending her into Joshua. He steadied her, so near that his breath fanned her, causing her heart to beat faster. She tilted her head to look him in the eye, and even though hundreds of people were around them, she felt no one's presence but his. He was a good, kind man who had been hurt terribly. That, they had in common. She lifted her hand to cup his jaw— strong, firm. Like the man himself.

"We're human. We make mistakes. We hopefully learn from those mistakes."

He veiled his expression. "I've learned to be very careful, not to rush into anything."

His warning, spoken in a harsh whisper, cautioned her to protect her heart. Falling in love with Joshua was a risk she wasn't willing to take. He wasn't ready for a relationship beyond friendship, and neither was she.

Darcy moved back and inhaled deeply to calm her rapidly beating heart. "I'd better get back. The afternoon auction will be starting in an hour and there are things to do."

"Can I help?"

"Surely you have something better to do than hang around a smelly barn?"

"No, I'm all yours for the afternoon."

His statement caused a hitch in her breathing. He meant nothing by that, but she began to dream of more. Her overriding thought was: How could Carol have betrayed him with another man?

Darcy headed toward the barn area, conscious of Joshua next to her. Halfway down the fairway she felt the hairs on the nape of her neck tingle. She scanned the crowd and stopped dead in her tracks when she saw Angus Feehan not three yards away, staring at her with narrowed eyes that transmitted his anger.

"What's wrong?" Joshua asked, moving to stand in front of her and blocking her view of the fired groom.

"Angus, behind you to the left."

Joshua glanced over his shoulder, stiffened and pivoted. He stalked toward the man. Angus's eyes widened, then he spun about and disappeared into the throng behind him. Joshua searched for a few minutes before returning to Darcy.

"I know this is a free country and he has every right to be here, but *why* is he here?" Darcy asked, hearing the panic in her voice.

"That was what I was going to ask him before he so conveniently vanished. Come on, let's get back to the barn." He placed his hand at the small of her back and guided her through the mass of people.

She heard raised voices coming from inside the barn where their horses were stabled for the auction. One, she knew, was her father's, and she quickened her pace. She found him arguing with Mike Reynolds, his arms waving as he spoke.

Shamus finished his tirade with "Get out before I call Security."

Mike lounged back against a stall. "Go ahead. I have every right to be here. This is public property and you can't order me off it."

Darcy stepped between the two men before they came to blows. "Dad, calm down. We aren't at Shamrock Stables." Then she turned to say to Mike, "Please go."

"Fine. But one day, old man, someone's going to knock you down a peg or two. You have no right to spread rumors about me."

"I'm only telling the truth. You shouldn't be around horses."

Darcy was glad she was standing between them, because she was sure if she hadn't been, they would have started a fistfight. She felt her father's tension and anger. She saw Mike's as he glared over her shoulder at her father. Mike huffed, then whirled about and stormed toward the entrance.

The tension remained. Darcy slowly pivoted toward her father, understanding where his anger was coming from, but realizing if he didn't control it, he would have another heart attack. "Dad, this isn't good for you."

"My heart's ticking just fine. I'm going to the arena to make sure everything is in place," he muttered, then stalked off in the opposite direction from Mike.

Joshua placed his hands on her shoulders and kneaded. "I don't think Mike Reynolds is capable of setting the fires."

"He isn't doing very well. He's lost several jobs because of the way he handles the horses. Maybe he blames the animals or the owners for his troubles."

"I suppose it's possible. He's certainly hotheaded enough, but it just doesn't feel right to me."

"I hope you find the person responsible soon. I don't know how much longer my father's going to be able to take this."

"Since everyone heightened security at the farms, there hasn't been a fire. And right now, with what we have, we don't have a suspect. I'll let the police know, though, about Angus showing up out here. It may be nothing—"

"Or it may be something. I want the person caught

but not at the expense of another fire. I guess there is no easy answer."

"Not with arson, I'm afraid."

Even though it was hot, Darcy felt cold to the bone. She and her father had their differences, but she was so afraid that if the arsonist wasn't caught soon, the stress would cause another heart attack.

Lord, please help my father deal with his anger better. Show me the way to help him and put a stop to this arsonist. I know I haven't prayed much in years, but I don't know what else to do anymore. He and Sean are all the family I have.

Darcy relaxed on a bale of hay that sat against the wall of the barn. The second day of the horse auction was over and it had gone very well. One more day and they would be finished with this big annual event. Her gaze swept the long aisle down the middle of the fairground barn, checking each stall that was occupied with a Shamrock Stables horse. One yearling stuck his head out, looking around. Several were eating. She heard the one in the last stall neighing. They had six horses left to auction off; two still had to be picked up by their new owners—they were the only animals in this barn. In the other two there were six farms represented, but Shamrock Stables was the biggest one at the county fair this year.

Everyone had worked overtime, especially her father, and she had volunteered to stay the night with the last batch of horses. Sean had wanted to join her, and she had decided at the last minute that he should go home with her father. He would have kept her up the whole night with his excitement. She couldn't afford to lose that sleep. Besides, it wasn't as if she was alone here. Every other farm had someone staying with their horses.

Darcy rose, stretched her cramped muscles and rolled her head in a full circle, trying to work the tension out. She walked to the door of the barn and looked out. She saw several grooms sitting under the large maple, talking and laughing. The noise from the fairway was diminishing as the crowd left for the evening.

Darkness had settled over the area where the barns were, but the lights from the fairway were a beacon in the night. Their brightness comforted her. Her last two years living at home, she had stayed with the horses at least one of the nights at the fair, but this year she felt edgy.

"Hi, Mrs. O'Brien. How's everything going?" One of the guards the farms had hired for the fair stopped in front of her.

"One more day and I can collapse."

"Have you even gone home since this began?"

"Yes, Friday evening."

"But you were here this morning at five, so you couldn't have been home for long."

"Just long enough to catch a few hours' sleep."

"Where are you sleeping tonight?"

"I'll be in the tack room if you need me."

"Except for a few teenagers who didn't go home when they were supposed to last night, it has been unusually quiet. Good night, Mrs. O'Brien." The guard ambled toward the next barn.

Darcy took a deep, fortifying breath and turned back into the barn. After walking its length and checking on the horses one final time, she made her way to the tack room, leaving the door open to give some light. Sitting in the corner was the cot her father had brought—a hard, uncomfortable cot with a thin blanket and a small pillow. Darcy eased down on it and listened carefully while untying her tennis shoes and removing them. The sounds of the fair were far away and faint.

Lying back, she threw the cover over herself and closed her eyes. The image of Joshua danced into her mind and brought a smile to her mouth. He had been wonderful this afternoon and evening, helping her with the horses and even bringing her something other than fattening food from the fairway to eat. The hot roast beef sandwich with cole slaw had been delicious. He was awfully good to her, she thought as she felt the effects of too little sleep. Joshua's image wavered and faded as sleep descended.

A horse's neigh pierced her dream. The scent of something burning accosted her. Darcy shot up, yanking off the blanket and surging to her feet. She rushed from the tack room into the main part of the barn; smoke billowed from the far end. The sounds of the frightened horses filled the air as quickly as the smoke did. Several were kicking their stalls. She saw one with wild eyes. She hurried to open the stall doors, trying her best not to breathe too deeply.

But still the smoke choked her as she reached the first stall. She coughed, placing her hand over her mouth and nose. Throwing the door open, she moved to the next one. She heard the horse bolting out. *One down, seven more to go.*

When she came to the fourth stall, she pulled the door open, but before she could get out of the way, the horse charged forward, the whites of his eyes all Darcy could focus on. He reared up and brought his hooves down, catching her on the shoulder. A sharp sensation like a knife cut shot through her, and she spun back against the wall. His front hooves came down again, clipping the side of her head. She sank to the dirt floor, pain radiating to every part of her. Through the smoke a man emerged, small and familiar looking, but Darcy had a hard time remembering who he was. His features wavered as she reached out to grasp him, to plead for his help. There was a searing pounding in her head as though someone were playing the bass drum inside her skull. Then darkness swallowed her up.

Chapter Eight

The insistent ringing of the phone invaded Joshua's dream about Darcy. He fumbled in the dark for the receiver, found it and brought it to his ear. "Yes."

"There's a fire at the fairgrounds. One of the barns. You need to get over there. I'm betting it's the work of the arsonist," his captain said, the sound of the sirens in the background.

"Are you on your way?" Joshua asked.

"Just about there. Get over here."

Joshua slammed the receiver down and jerked back the covers. Five minutes later, dressed in jeans and a T-shirt, he raced for his truck, fear gripping him so hard that his heart hammered against his rib cage. Darcy was in one of those barns. *Please, Lord, let her be okay.*

Thankfully there was little traffic at midnight. He sped toward the fairgrounds, thoughts of Darcy trapped in a burning barn spurring him to drive faster than was safe.

* * *

Darcy's head throbbed; every part of her was sore. A cool breeze brushed her face. When she opened her eyes, she saw that she was outside the barn, at the back, a few feet from the entrance. In the distance she heard the wail of sirens. Closer, the frantic shouts of several people and the smoke-filled air reminded her of the fire.

She started to rise and her vision blurred. Squeezing her eyes closed for a few precious seconds, she held her head, trying not to breathe too deeply. Then she attempted again to stand, this time more slowly. Her head still pulsated with pain, but she dismissed it. She had to get back inside and make sure all the horses got out.

With her gaze trained on the flames licking their way toward the back of the barn, Darcy darted inside toward the nearest stall. Nausea rose up in her and she swayed. Gripping the nearest thing, a pole, she stopped to get her bearings. She couldn't see beyond a few feet as the smoke thickened.

Please, Lord, help me rescue the horses.

The sounds of frenzied horses propelled her forward. She reached the nearest stall and swung the door open. Moving as fast as her throbbing head would allow, she got out of the way of the charging horse. It disappeared out the back door. Hugging low to the ground, she felt along the wall to the next stall and thrust it open. Plastered against the side, she watched that yearling escape to safety. She repeated the same actions at the next one.

Over the noise of the firefighters arriving and the fire

engulfing the wooden structure, she heard her name being shouted. *Joshua.* "Over here."

He appeared through the haze, dressed in jeans and a T-shirt, but with a mask and helmet on his head. In his right hand he carried an extra set. He immediately thrust the helmet and mask toward her and helped her to put it on. "Come on. You're getting out of here. The fire is out of control. It won't be long until this whole building goes," he shouted through the mask. He gripped her arm.

"No. Can't yet," she rasped, her throat burning with the effort to speak.

She only had one more stall. She wrenched herself from his grasp and started for it. Her eyes stung, her lungs seared as though the fire consumed her. But she thought she could make it and still get out. Three feet. Two.

A crashing sound behind her sped her heart to a thundering pace. She glanced over her shoulder and saw Joshua right behind her. Beyond him part of the roof near the front had fallen. A shudder ripped down her length.

"Get out. I'll get the horse." His voice vibrated with his anger. "*Now,* Darcy." He shoved her toward the rear door, not giving her a chance to think or respond.

She started back to help him—it wasn't his animal— but hands grabbed her and pulled her from the barn. Two firefighters headed into the blaze; a third, Ned, indicated she should move away from the building.

Darcy stared at the entrance, the images swimming

before her eyes. She *couldn't* pass out. She had to make sure Joshua made it out. He was in there because of her. When she spied the last horse racing from the barn followed by Joshua, she sank to the ground, her legs no longer able to support her. Her whole body shook from exhaustion and spent adrenaline. Her stomach roiled; her lungs felt tight, the last good breaths squeezed from them. Ripping off the helmet and mask, she began to cough.

Across the smoky expanse, Joshua's gaze connected with hers. He walked toward her, anger marking his features and his long strides. She blinked. There were two of him, then three. The throbbing in her head intensified and each breath hurt. She cradled her face, her fingers touching a sticky substance where the horse had kicked her.

Blackness nibbled at her consciousness. She blinked again, trying to calm her reeling stomach, to push away the dark mist before her eyes.

"I can't believe you did that, Darcy," Joshua said, halting in front of her, his legs planted a foot apart, his hands on his hips.

She made the mistake of tilting her head back to peer up into his face. The blackness gobbled her up once more.

Anger gripped Joshua so tightly his muscles hurt. He stared down at Darcy, wanting to shake some sense into her. She could have died in that fire. He could take risks. She couldn't! She closed her eyes, heaved a deep breath and fell over. He stooped to catch her in his arms.

Cradling her against his chest, he felt his rage slip from him. All his thoughts were centered on getting help for Darcy. She'd been inside too long. He brushed her hair away from her face and discovered blood oozing from a wound on the side of her head. His heart plummeted.

Dear Heavenly Father, please don't let her die.

Joshua shouted for help while laying her back on the hard ground. One of the paramedics rushed over and kneeled to check her.

Stan glanced at Joshua. "Smoke inhalation and most likely a concussion. We'll transport her to the hospital."

While Stan fetched the stretcher, Joshua stayed next to Darcy. His eyes burned from the smoke and something else he didn't want to think about. They were friends. That was all. Hadn't he told himself that enough times over the past few weeks? But…he didn't want anything to happen to her.

Joshua touched her dirt-smudged face, brushing his fingers over her skin. He laid his palm against the curve of her jaw and remembered her laughter. When she smiled, his whole world brightened to the point that it scared him.

Stan, accompanied by another paramedic, returned and they transferred Darcy to the stretcher. Joshua walked with her, holding her hand even though she had not awakened.

At the ambulance Stan asked, "Coming with us or staying?"

Torn between his duty and desire, Joshua stared at

his friend, trying to decide what he should do. He had to stay. Everything inside of him demanded he do what he was good at and find the person behind the fires, and yet he didn't want to leave Darcy's side, even though there was nothing he could do for her at the hospital. He could, however, gather information and evidence to track down the arsonist before someone died. That *had* to be his priority.

He knew he had to remain at the fire; in his heart he would go with Darcy, at least in spirit, and he would pray for her fast recovery until he could be with her.

"I'm staying. Let me know what the doctor says, Stan."

"Will do." Stan peered at the barn, partially destroyed by the flames. "It looks like we'll be able to contain the fire to just this one barn. That's good news."

"Thank goodness there wasn't any wind this evening and someone quickly called in the fire."

"I'll take care of her. You go do your magic."

Joshua watched the ambulance pull away from the barn area, his heart heavy, his thoughts with Darcy. *Lord, I need Your help. Who is burning these barns? Why? Please guide me to the truth. I don't want to see anyone else get hurt. Please watch over Darcy for me and heal her. Be with her.*

The pounding in her head threatened to overwhelm Darcy and push her back into the darkness. She felt something over her mouth and wondered if she still had the mask on. No, she'd tossed it on the ground.

Noises, people's voices, machines beeping and an antiseptic smell dragged her toward consciousness. She eased her eyes open.

Pale-blue walls met her inspection. A television was mounted on a shelf high in the corner. A sound to her left shifted her attention in that direction. Her father, his eyes closed, sat on the small tan sofa with Sean curled up asleep, cradled against his grandfather's side. In a chair next to the bed sat Joshua, his chin resting on his chest, his body completely relaxed in sleep.

She was in a hospital room, and from the looks of the bright sunlight streaming through the partially opened drapes it was probably late morning. Did all the horses make it? Were the firefighters able to save the other barns? Questions inundated her, demanding answers.

She removed the oxygen mask from her face and nudged Joshua's hand, which rested near hers on the bed. He stirred, lifting his head to snare her with his tired eyes. A smile tugged at the corners of his mouth, kicking her heartbeat into a faster tempo.

"I'm not sure if I should yell at you or kiss you."

"Well, if you want my opinion, I would prefer a kiss," Darcy said, her voice raw as though she hadn't used it in a long time. Her throat hurt as much as her head.

She leaned toward the bedside table to get the pitcher and pour herself some water. Joshua motioned her back and poured it for her. He supported her while she took several long sips, soothing her searing throat. His scent of musk played havoc with her senses. He was so near she could even smell his mint-flavored toothpaste. Visions of that kiss he'd mentioned danced in her mind.

When she was through drinking, he placed the glass close to her on the table. "You shouldn't have gone back in after the horses. You were lucky."

"I know, but I couldn't stand by and listen to the horses dying."

His eyes gentled. "I know." He covered her hand with his. "But you almost died last night. You gave me quite a scare."

"You weren't exactly easy on me. I thought I might never see you again when the last horse came out and you didn't."

"I wasn't far behind him."

"Those seconds seemed like an eternity."

"Then you know what I went through when I called your name and you didn't respond."

"But I did."

"Not at first. An eternity passed before I heard you."

"Mom, you're okay?" Sean asked, hopping up from the couch and rushing toward her. He threw his arms around her and hugged her. "I was so worried."

Darcy caught Joshua's "I told you so" look while she pressed her son close to her heart. Her father moved slower toward the bed, his face haggard, exhaustion evident in his expression. He bent down and kissed her on the cheek.

"Child, don't ever give us that kind of scare again. I can replace the horses. I can't replace you."

Darcy's mouth fell open. In her heart she knew her father loved her, but he never said anything to her about his feelings. There had been times she had felt the farm was more important to him than she was. For him to say otherwise made her throat constrict. She reached for the glass and took another sip to ease the tightness.

"Did all the horses make it?"

"Yes," her father answered, stepping back to sit again on the couch.

Sean bounced onto the end of the bed. "Grandpa found the last one early this morning. Only one was injured but not seriously. I helped look for the horses."

Darcy smiled at her son. "You're becoming quite a little helper."

He puffed out his chest. "I'm not little. Grandpa said so."

"How are the other barns?"

"No damage. The firefighters were able to confine the fire to that one barn." Joshua leaned back in his chair. "Can you tell me what happened?"

Darcy touched her head where her wound was and winced. There was something at the edges of her mind that she knew was important. She closed her eyes and concentrated on the events of the past evening. What was she forgetting?

"I was asleep in the tack room when I heard something—the horses, I believe." She rubbed her forehead. *Think!* "I went out into the barn and saw the smoke. I immediately started opening the stall doors. One horse caught me with his front hooves. I went down. I—" A vague image wavered like a highway on a hot day. "I blacked out."

"In the barn?" Joshua asked, sitting forward, his elbows resting on his thighs.

"Yes, but when I woke up I was outside. Someone must have dragged me from the barn. I—" Again a featureless face materialized in her mind. She stared into space and tried to put details on that face. "I remember a man bending over me in the barn."

"Who?" Her father came to the bed again, hovering over her, his expression intense.

"I—I've seen the man before. He was small, dark hair."

"Angus. I knew it!" Her father slapped his hand against his leg. "He had no reason to be there unless he was up to no good."

She shook her head and regretted it the second she did. The pounding intensified. "Not Angus." Slowly she pieced together the image of the man leaning over her, smoke surrounding them. "I think…it was…" Slowly the haze lifted even more and features swirled into a picture of a man. "Tom Bolton."

Joshua bolted to his feet. "Are you sure?"

"I think so."

"One of the grooms saw a small man running away. He couldn't catch the man." Joshua headed for the door.

"Where are you going, son?"

"To have a little chat with Tom. It's time this stops."

The controlled anger in Joshua's voice made Darcy shudder.

* * *

Despite faint throbbing against her skull, Darcy paced from one end of her living room to the other. Joshua had said he would be here by now. She wanted to know what had happened when he talked with Tom. Other than to tell her that Tom had admitted to setting the fires, Joshua hadn't given her any details.

Her father came into the room. "Darcy, I promised the doctor you would rest. That's the only reason the doctor let you come home today. Sit. Joshua will be here when he can make it."

She pivoted toward her father, frowning. "I knew Tom Bolton was angry about his daughter's accident— but to do what he did? I don't understand."

"Grief can make a person do many things they wouldn't normally do."

Darcy wondered about the tone in her father's voice. He spoke as though he knew from experience. Was it grief over her mother's suicide he was talking about? Or grief because her mother hadn't been "normal" for much of their marriage? Darcy could still remember her mother's highs, but especially her lows, which had become more frequent as the years passed. Why hadn't her father been able to help her mother? That question she had wanted him to answer for a long time, but she'd never had the nerve to ask.

The doorbell chimed. Ignoring the pain in her head as much as possible, Darcy hurried to answer it. She threw open the door and smiled at the wonderful sight of Joshua standing on the porch. "It's about time."

"I'm only a few minutes—" he checked his watch "—okay, half an hour late. May I come in?"

She laughed and stepped to the side. "Of course. What happened when you went to see Tom? Why did he do it?"

Joshua held up his hand. "Whoa, Darcy. Let's go into the living room and sit. You should be resting. It isn't every day you get a concussion."

"You just want to drive me crazy."

Joshua waved his hand toward the living room. "My lips are sealed until you're sitting."

"Between you and Dad I'm gonna have more than my share of resting," she muttered, making her way back into the living room and sitting on the couch. She knew they were right, but waiting for Joshua had taxed her patience.

"Good evening, sir. I see you've had your hands full."

"I think she comes by it honestly. I'm not the best patient in the world, either."

"Right," Darcy interjected. "Okay, I'm sitting. Now, tell me everything."

"I found Tom at home. I think he was expecting me."

"Because I saw him."

"His hatred for horses sent him over the edge. All he could think of was to destroy every one he could. The more he was around Crystal the more angry he got about her accident, to the point he decided to set the barns on fire. I think, though, your injury last night sobered him to what he was doing."

"He didn't have to drag me from the barn. He knew I saw him, and by helping me to escape the fire he was sealing his own fate."

"He told me the fires were about hurting what had hurt his daughter. Nothing else but that. He never wanted anyone to get hurt. That's why they were always at night when people weren't around."

"Also a good time to conceal one's movements," her father said with a snort.

Darcy sighed. "It's over. That's the main thing."

"What's sad is that I don't think Tom thought beyond his actions to what it would do to his family. When the police took Tom away, Tanya and Crystal were sobbing. I stayed to try and calm them down before giving them a ride to the police station."

"Oh, my. What will this do to them?" Darcy covered her mouth with her hand, thinking back to the times she had talked to Crystal and Tanya. They both had so many problems—and now this. "Are they still at the station?"

"No, they should be home by now. Reverend Collins came down to the police station and was going to take them home."

Darcy rose. "Will you take me to see Tanya?"

"Darcy, I don't think that's a good idea," her father said, standing too, and moving toward the entrance as though to block her exit.

"She needs a friend right now and I intend to help her and Crystal as much as possible. In fact, I think Sean should come along and bring Lady to help cheer up Crystal."

"But you're the reason Tom is in jail right now," her father said.

"I am not. *Tom* is the reason he is in jail. I want Tanya to know that I have no hard feelings toward her."

Her father's gaze pinned her. "But she may toward you."

"I still have to try to help."

Joshua came up beside her. "If I don't take you, are you going to try to drive yourself?"

She lifted her chin, determined to challenge both her father and Joshua if need be. In the past she wouldn't have, but she was discovering the power of standing up for what she believed in. And she believed that Tanya and Crystal needed her to be a friend.

"If I have to."

"Then I'll take you. Where's Sean?" Joshua asked, touching the small of her back.

The feel of his fingers honed her senses to him. She liked knowing he would be accompanying her, because she wasn't sure how Tanya would receive her. Joshua gave her the strength to do what was right.

"He's out back, trying to teach Lady some tricks."

"Lady is only seven weeks old."

"Yeah, I know. She's constantly moving. He has a hard time getting her attention."

"She'll calm down as she grows older."

"I hope so."

"I'll get Sean and Lady. Stay here until I return."

"Aye, aye, captain."

Joshua gave her an exasperated look at the entrance into the kitchen. "I mean it, Darcy. No trying to walk to the truck by yourself. Guard her, Shamus."

Her father chuckled. "Little does he know how useless that would be. Doesn't he know by now when you're determined to do something you will do it?"

"It didn't use to be like that."

"True, child, but you've changed since you got married."

"No, Dad, I changed after Clay died. What you see is the new me."

"I like it. What made you change?"

She held a deep breath for a few seconds before blowing it out through pursed lips. "I got tired of suppressing who I really was."

"Who is that?"

"I'm a work in progress at the moment. But I do know I won't keep my opinion to myself any longer."

"Tell me something I don't know."

"Grandpa, Lady sat for me."

"She did? For how long?"

"Maybe two seconds."

"I think you need to work on that trick," her father said, ruffling Sean's red hair. "In order for that to work she needs to stay seated until you tell her to move. But I do like how she's beginning to walk on a leash."

While Sean raced ahead with Lady yelping at his heels, Joshua wound his arm about Darcy's shoulders and led her to the truck.

"I can't wait to show Crystal my new trick with Lady. When she gets her own dog, I can help her train it."

"By the time she gets a dog, we may be back in Panama City."

"Oh, I forgot. Well, next summer I can help her."

On the ride to the Boltons', Darcy thought about her home in Panama City that she had been painstakingly renovating—the first one she'd spent any time on in the ten years since she'd left here. Strange, she really didn't remember much about her home and the plans she had had for it. In a short time the farm had become her home again. But the last time she'd lived here she'd lost who she was. She was determined for that not to happen again—even if it meant staying away from Shamrock Stables.

Joshua escorted her to the Boltons' front door, his arm steady about her. She liked its feel about her. Comforting. Sheltering. Like the man.

Tanya answered the doorbell immediately as though she had been expecting them. She took one look at Darcy and began to cry, throwing herself at her. Darcy hugged the woman as she sobbed against her shoulder.

"I'm so sorry to hear about Tom. I wanted to offer you my help if you'll take it." Darcy patted Tanya on the back while Sean, Lady and Joshua went into the house.

"I can't believe you're here. I thought you would hate us for what Tom nearly did to you. I'm the one who is sorry. I should have known what he was doing and made him stop. Crystal's beside herself. She has been crying all day and I can't seem to stop. What am I going to do? How will I be able to hold my head up in this town after what Tom did?"

It was Darcy's turn to clasp Tanya against her and walk into her house. "You did nothing wrong. No one's going to blame you or Crystal. I certainly don't."

Tanya's tears continued to fall unchecked down her cheeks. "All I want to do is stay in this house and never see anyone. I can't face people. I can't deal with it."

"Have you taken your medication today?" Darcy asked, remembering Tanya talking about how stressed she had been to the point of forgetting to take her medicine. From her own experience with her mother, Darcy knew that would only make the situation worse.

Tanya paused in the middle of the living room and thought for a moment. "No, I forgot."

"That's the first thing you should do. Then we'll sit in the kitchen and discuss your situation over a cup of coffee. I can make some while you're taking your medicine."

While Tanya went to get her medication, Darcy walked into the kitchen and found the counters littered with dirty dishes. She saw the coffeepot next to the sink. After washing it out, she put some coffee on to brew, then set about tidying up while she waited for Tanya to return.

Ten minutes later Tanya appeared in the doorway, her face blotchy as though she had been crying again. "I'm sorry. I took one look at myself in the mirror and broke down."

"Did you get your medicine?" Darcy asked, rinsing off the last plate to go into the dishwasher.

She held up the bottle, then opened it and poured one pill into her palm. "I know this place looks a mess, but I've been so preoccupied I haven't gotten a chance to clean up." Tanya took a glass and filled it with water, then downed her medicine.

"That's why I'm here. To help. You sit while I finish up."

"But you were just in the hospital. You shouldn't be doing anything."

Darcy motioned with her hand, dismissing Tanya's concern. "I'm fine. Besides, all I'm doing is running some water over a few dishes. Not very taxing." With the last pot in the dishwasher, she closed it, then turned slowly to face Tanya, making sure she didn't move suddenly. Her medication was helping the pain but not totally. The scent of brewing coffee saturated the air. "How do you like your coffee?"

"Black."

Darcy served Tanya her cup, then got one for herself, putting in several spoons of sugar. "The sweeter the better." When she sat across from Tanya, she continued, "Have you got a lawyer to represent Tom?"

Tanya stared at her cup.

"Tanya, do you have a lawyer?"

The woman blinked, jerking her head up. "Yes. There won't be a lengthy trial, though, since he confessed. He told me that seeing you on the ground in the barn last night shook him up, brought him to his senses.

He'd never meant for a person to get hurt. He's a good man. Really."

Darcy bit her lower lip to keep from pointing out that hurting animals wasn't okay. In her mind she felt Tom had gone a bit crazy with his daughter's accident. "Grief can do strange things to some people."

"How are Crystal and I going to live? I don't have a job. We have so many bills to pay."

"As soon as you feel up to it, I can help you with a résumé." Darcy took a sip of her coffee. "Also, Joshua and Sean want to build that ramp for Crystal so she can enjoy the backyard. What do you say?"

"I don't want to be any trouble to anyone." Tanya ran her finger around the rim of her cup, her gaze focused on its black contents.

"It looks like Sean and Lady were just what Crystal needed." Joshua entered the kitchen and took the chair next to Darcy. "I left those two laughing at Lady's attempt to roll over—or I guess more accurately, Sean's attempt to teach her a new trick."

"That's good," Tanya murmured, never lifting her gaze to Joshua.

Darcy caught his attention and shrugged. "When do you think you can start on the ramp?"

"How about Wednesday afternoon, Tanya?"

"Fine."

The listless tone in Tanya's voice worried Darcy, but she didn't know what to do. While Joshua entertained them with a description of Sean's training technique, Darcy prayed to God for guidance in helping Tanya. It had been years since she had turned to the Lord for assistance, but no matter how independent she wanted to be, she was learning her limits. Since her return home, she was quietly discovering there were some problems only the Lord could help with.

Weariness wore her down. By the time Joshua was finished with his story, Darcy didn't even have the strength to lift her cup. She had overextended herself today.

Joshua searched her features and frowned. He rose. "We'd better be going. It's been a long day for everyone."

After retrieving Sean and Lady, he escorted Darcy to his truck. His arm about her was what kept her standing.

"I'm gonna have to learn to say no to you," he whispered close to her ear.

Her neck tingled from the caress of his words. "I didn't leave you much of a choice."

"True. But you need your rest so you can help Sean and me with the ramp."

"If you could see me with a hammer, you wouldn't even suggest that."

"But I bet you'll look cute in a tool belt."

She laughed. "You stole my line."

"Come Wednesday we'll have to let Crystal and Sean decide who looks the best wearing a tool belt." He assisted her into his truck, his hand lingering on her arm longer than necessary.

He stared into her eyes for several moments, warmth

and friendship offered. Then his look evolved into something beyond friendship, and her pulse rate sped. Hope flared for a heartbeat, until she thought of all the obstacles in their way. She wasn't even sure who she was. How could she ask someone to love her when she was changing? How could she love someone when she didn't know what she really wanted?

Chapter Nine

"We'll need to go get the supplies, then pick up Sean at Jesse and Nate's." Darcy climbed into Joshua's truck, looking forward to spending some time with him. The past few days, all she'd thought about was Joshua coming to her rescue in the burning barn or Joshua touching her on the hand or smiling at her with his whole face alight even down to a twinkle in his blue eyes.

"How are you feeling?"

"Much better. The headache's only a faint throb, barely noticeable."

"That's good. Don't give me a fright like that again." His expression set in a frown, Joshua threw the truck into drive and pulled away from her house.

"Where do you suggest we get the lumber for the ramp?"

"The best prices in town are at Northland Lumber."

"Isn't that a new store near the renovated downtown area?"

"Yes."

The clipped answer concerned Darcy. Was he still angry at her for taking a risk when rescuing the horses? Or was it something else? She twisted about, searching Joshua's face.

"What aren't you telling me?"

His frown deepened to a scowl. "Carol's married to the manager of Northland."

"Then we don't have to go there."

"No, I need to move on. I can't avoid going to Northland because of my ex-fiancée, especially since it's the best chance to get all the supplies in one store." He glanced at her. "I've heard that Carol wants to return to Sweetwater Community Church."

"And how do you feel about that?"

He gripped the steering wheel tighter, tension visibly moving from his face to flood his whole body. "It's one thing to see the happy family occasionally, but a completely different thing to run into them every week at church, a place I consider my sanctuary."

"Maybe she won't attend the same service as you."

"Maybe" was his tight comment.

Compelled to comfort him, Darcy laid her hand on his arm, wishing she had the right to do more. So many times he'd been there for her. "I know what it feels like to be hurt by someone you love. It knocks the breath out of you."

"It's hard to acknowledge you could have been so wrong about a person."

"Shakes your confidence in your ability to choose wisely."

"Right." His hands about the steering wheel relaxed, the rigid set to his shoulders eased.

"I've been in your shoes. I know what you're going through." *I'm still going through it,* Darcy amended silently. She wasn't entirely over her disastrous marriage to Clay. The effects of doubting her choices lingered and colored every judgment she made. She wasn't sure that would ever totally change.

"I knew there was a reason I liked you." He shifted his full attention to her while waiting at a stoplight.

Okay, she knew it was dangerous to feel warm and fuzzy, but she did. He made her feel special as no man ever had. Totally dangerous—their conversation about Carol only confirmed it. He wasn't over his ex-fiancée, might still be in love with her, even if he didn't acknowledge that to himself. Why else would he be so upset more than a year later?

Joshua parked in the lot in front of Northland Lumber. For a few seconds he just sat in the truck, staring at the entrance as though he expected Carol to come out and greet him. Darcy's throat contracted, her mouth went dry. She wanted to help him move on for a purely selfish reason. She cared about Joshua Markham.

"Were you friends with her husband?"

His jaws clenched. He sighed heavily. "Yes. We weren't best friends or anything like that, but I knew him. We used to play on a softball team together before I got so busy I had to quit. I think that's how she met him."

"You haven't forgiven her, have you?"

His jawline hardened even more. "I'm trying. Most of the time I don't think about it. Lately I have been."

"Why now?"

Switching off the engine, he shifted so he faced her with only a foot between them. "You. You make me think of things that I'd decided might not be in my future."

The breath bottled in her lungs burned. "You know I'm as leery as you are of moving our relationship forward."

"Yes. I know why I feel that way. Why do you?"

"My marriage wasn't a partnership. I found myself suffocating. I worked hard to make sure nothing rocked the boat with Clay, and that can be very exhausting." There was so much more to the story than that, but Darcy still wasn't ready to confess all her mixed up feelings to someone she hadn't known but a month. She and Clay had dated for a year and a half, and look what happened to that relationship. "I'm trying to discover who the real Darcy O'Brien is."

"I can tell you what I see. I see a person who is loving and caring, who is determined to do the right thing, who has taken a woman under her wing whose husband nearly killed her."

The warm, fuzzy feeling spread from the pit of her stomach to encompass her whole body. She wished she deserved his praise. "I'm helping Tanya because she is bipolar. My mother was bipolar and I want to understand the illness. As a teenager I didn't."

"So that's the only reason we're going shopping for some lumber to build a ramp? You could look the illness up on the Internet if that was all. Don't sell yourself short, Darcy."

He brushed a strand of her hair back behind her ear. The feather-soft touch curled her toes. "I couldn't help my mother. Maybe I can help Tanya. But my relationship with my mother isn't the point of this conversation."

He arched a brow. "It isn't?"

"No, we were talking about you forgiving Carol. The man I know doesn't usually hold grudges."

"I'd built in my mind my whole future around Carol. When she married Kyle, everything fell apart." He yanked his door open. "We'd better get moving if we're going to build this ramp today."

Inside the store the tension returned to Joshua's features. At any second Darcy was sure she would run into Carol coming around the next corner. When they left thirty minutes later, she hadn't even met Kyle, Carol's husband. For several miles on the drive to Nate's Joshua still held himself rigid, but slowly the tension slipped from him. Darcy breathed a sigh of relief.

After picking up Sean at Nate's, the three of them headed to the Boltons'. As she walked up to the house, Darcy wondered what kind of reception they would receive. With Tanya she never knew how she would be from one hour to the next—much like her mother had been.

Tanya threw open the door before Joshua had a

chance to ring the bell. "You all are *finally* here. Crystal has been at the window for the past hour, waiting for you to come. Come in, come in."

Joshua snagged Darcy's look, his brows raised. Darcy entered while Joshua and Sean went back to the truck to begin to unload the supplies. Darcy greeted Crystal.

"I want to watch them work. Can I sit out on the deck, Mom?"

"Sure, sweetie. Be a sec, Darcy. I have some things I want to show you." Tanya rolled her daughter toward the kitchen.

After only being gone a moment, Tanya bounced back into the room, a smile on her face and an almost wild look in her eyes. "Come on back to my bedroom. I can't wait to show you what I bought."

With hesitation Darcy followed the woman in the opposite direction from the kitchen. "I'm gonna help the guys with the ramp."

"Oh, this will only take a sec." When Tanya stepped into her bedroom, she swept her arm toward the bed. "They were all on sale. I couldn't resist."

Covering the bed were mounds of clothes with the price tags still on them. On the floor nearby were ten boxes of shoes. Darcy's mouth fell open. She brought her hand up to cover her surprise.

"I thought I should go shopping for some new clothes for any job interviews I'll have. You've got to look your best if you want the job. I so appreciate you helping me with the résumé. With your help and these new clothes I'll have a job in no time, and Crystal and I won't have a worry."

Tanya talked a mile a minute. Darcy had a hard time following her conversation. She blinked and tried to focus on what the woman was saying, but all she saw was the thousands of dollars' worth of clothes on the bed—thousands of dollars that Tanya didn't have.

"What do you think?" Tanya held up a red suit, conservatively cut, and a pair of matching heels.

"Nice, but do you really need all these outfits?"

"Sure. They're perfect." Tanya took a dress from the pile and fingered the silky blue material.

"Have you taken your medication today?"

"I don't need that. I'm doing fine, Darcy. Crystal's gonna have the ramp she's wanted, the lawyer thinks that Tom can cut a deal with the district attorney because of the unusual circumstances surrounding the case. And the day is gorgeous. Great day to build a ramp. Let's go help." Tanya started for the door.

Darcy blocked her escape. "When was the last time you saw your doctor?"

"I don't need to see a doctor. I'm feeling great." Tanya pushed past Darcy and hurried down the hall.

Darcy stared at the bed and shook her head. A memory intruded: her mother standing out in front of the house while Hanson Furniture Store delivered several rooms' worth of new furniture that they had no need for and no place to put. Her mother had gone to the store for a new chair for the den and had bought thousands and thousands of dollars' worth of pieces that her father had had to return the next day—after a terrible argument between him and her mother.

When Darcy joined everyone out back, the first thing she noticed was Tanya flittering from Crystal to Joshua and Sean then back to her daughter. The woman couldn't seem to stay still. All her activity made Darcy tired just looking at her.

"Hey, I could use some help over here," Joshua called out to Darcy.

She pushed away from the door frame she'd been leaning against and made her way toward him. His gaze flickered to Tanya then back to Darcy.

"Is everything all right with Tanya?" he asked, handing her some nails to hold for him.

"No. I don't think she's taking her medicine very regularly. She's in one of her manic stages."

"You think? I believe she could climb the side of the house and not blink an eye."

Darcy peered at Crystal, who watched her mother buzz about the deck, constantly in motion but not accomplishing anything. The worried look on the child's face reminded Darcy of what she'd gone through as a child, observing her mother's bizarre behavior and not understanding.

"Sean, can you help Joshua over here?"

Her son finished stacking the lumber and hurried to her. "You bet. When do I get to hammer?"

While Joshua showed Sean what to do, Darcy strode to Crystal and pulled up a chair next to her. Tanya had disappeared inside the house. "How are you doing?"

"Okay."

If the sound of Crystal's voice was any indication, the young girl wasn't doing okay. "If something's bothering you, maybe I can help."

Her brow wrinkled, the child turned toward Darcy. "Did Mom show you her new clothes?"

"Yes."

"She got me a whole bunch of new outfits, too. I don't need any. I don't go too many places."

"Maybe your mother can take them back tomorrow."

"Maybe." Crystal studied her hands laced together in her lap.

"I'll talk with your mom and see what I can do."

"Thanks, Darcy. Is Sean going to Vacation Bible School next week?"

"You bet. That's all he's talked about lately. Are you?"

Crystal looked toward the back door. "I don't know."

"Do you want me to ask your mother if I can pick you up and take you with Sean?"

Crystal's eyes brightened. "Will you…just in case she isn't feeling too well?"

"Sure. I hear at the end they're going to have a talent show for anyone who wants to participate. Sean's talking about singing. He says you sing well. Maybe you two can do a duet."

"Me sing in front of people? I don't know about that."

"You might want to think about it. Sean's planning on asking his grandfather to come and see him perform. He might need some moral support." Especially if he couldn't get his grandpa to attend, Darcy thought. She was afraid Sean was in for a disappointment when he asked.

"I'll be there for moral support in the audience."

"Then you can sit next to me and hold my hand, because I'm going to be one nervous mother."

The child's laughter rang out, the sound a welcome change from the tension churning in the air. "You don't need me. You can do anything. Sean says so."

Embarrassment heated Darcy's cheeks. "I wish that were true. We all have our strengths and our weaknesses."

Again Crystal's gaze drifted to the back door. "Yes, I guess we do."

Darcy wanted to take the young girl into her embrace and tell her not to blame herself for her mother's illness, to seek help if she needed it. She wished she had.

"I wish I could go, Sean, but I'll be too busy that evening." Shamus spooned some oatmeal into his bowl, frowning at the cereal. "Why is the food that's good for you so bad tasting?" he mumbled, plopping the spoon back into the serving dish.

"Grandpa, you've got to come."

"No, I don't, my boy."

"But *everyone* is gonna be there. I'm singing."

"I can hear you sing here at the farm." Darcy's father poured milk onto his oatmeal, his nose wrinkling.

Darcy's stomach knotted. Sitting across from her

son, she could clearly see his disappointment. He had been counting on his grandfather coming to see him. She'd tried to warn Sean that he probably wouldn't, but her son wouldn't listen to her. Her own disappointment took hold of her, forging a determination to have a word with her father after Sean left to do his chores.

Silence reigned at the dining room table. A heavy, taut silence. Darcy forced herself to eat a few bites of the oatmeal, but it settled like a lump in her stomach. She gave up trying to eat.

As soon as Sean finished his cereal, he jumped to his feet, then remembered to ask, "May I be excused?"

"Yes, honey. I'll be ready to take you to Vacation Bible School in an hour."

Without a word or look toward his grandfather, Sean raced from the room.

"Does that child know what walking is?"

"Yes, Dad." She cleared her throat, her hands twisting together in her lap. "Please reconsider going to the talent show. It's not really going to church."

"Didn't you tell me there was a service before the show?"

"Yes, but you can come late."

"Humph. I vowed I wouldn't set foot in that church after your mother died."

Darcy tossed her napkin on the table and straightened in her chair, preparing to do battle. "Why, Dad? You never told me why."

"Because it is none—" He clamped his mouth down on the last part of the sentence and glared at her. Then, with a deep breath, he continued. "God let me down. For years I was a good Christian who went to church every Sunday. All I asked of the Lord was to heal Nancy, to give my wife back to me. That didn't happen, so I stopped going."

"You can't bargain with God. He knows what's best, and sometimes we just have to accept what He plans for us rather than what we plan for ourselves."

"Is that what you really feel?"

A calm settled over Darcy, and for the first time she realized the true meaning of giving herself totally to the Lord, with no strings attached. "Yes. I know how important control is to you, but we can't control everything."

Her father splayed his hand over his heart. "I know that. These past few months have clearly shown me my limitations."

"Make your grandson happy. Come hear him sing. We don't have a big family. We need to stick together."

"Do you really feel that way?"

She nodded.

"Then why were you gone for ten years? That's not sticking together, child."

"I was wrong."

Her father shoved his chair back and stood. "No, you were angry at me and I think you still are."

Darcy came to her feet, not wanting to give her father a height advantage. Every part of her rang with her anger. "Yes, I was—I still am."

"Why?"

That one word sent the tension in the room skyrocketing. "Because you're the reason Mother killed herself."

Her father's eyes widened, then fury chased away his surprise and settled over his features. "How dare you say that! I loved your mother very much."

"Then why were you two always fighting? Why did she spend most of her days in her room, sleeping or crying, that last year? Why didn't you help her?"

He clenched his hands at his sides. "Because she wouldn't take her medication and refused to see the doctor. No matter how much I pleaded, I couldn't get her to do anything to help herself. People have to want to help themselves or nothing you do will matter." He covered the short space between them. "Why do you think I turned to the Lord? I couldn't help her. I thought maybe He could. He didn't."

A vision of her mother the last time she'd seen her flashed into her mind. "I found her, Dad, that morning, lying on her bed as though she were asleep, peaceful, except she wouldn't wake up. That's when I found the bottle of her medication by her nightstand, completely empty. I knew then that she'd taken the whole prescription at once. You never said a word to me about it. You just locked yourself in your office and worked. I *needed* you." Her whole body shook with her intense emotions, with the pain of remembering, with the image that plagued her to this day.

"Not the way I was after your mother died. I wasn't good for anyone. I lost the woman I loved and I blamed

God. But mostly I blamed myself. I should have been able to do something."

"So instead, you turned away from me *and* God."

"Don't you see, Darcy, I was never any good at words. I couldn't explain how I was feeling, let alone explain anything to you."

"How about a simple, 'I love you, Darcy.' That's all I needed. That's all I ever needed to hear from you." *And never did,* she thought, tension gripping her stomach.

"I do."

"You have a funny way of showing it. You can't even say the words now." Her true feelings, bottled up for years, spewed forward, and while a part of Darcy was taken by surprise, another part was not at all surprised. She was learning to say what she felt. He started to speak, and she cut him off, continuing. "You always demanded I do everything perfectly. I have a news flash for you, Dad, people aren't perfect. But I tried my best. And I always felt I let you down. If you must know, that's the real reason I stayed away for ten years. I couldn't stand to see the disappointment in your eyes one more time. I had all I could handle with trying to keep my marriage together with a man who was as demanding and controlling as you were. Never again."

Her father took several steps back, a sheen to his eyes. "Why didn't you say something before now?"

"Don't you dare turn everything back on me. I shouldn't have had to say anything. You're my father. You should love me without putting conditions on that love. You should love the Lord the same way." The force of her anger prodded her toward the door of the dining room. She needed to get out of here, the air hot and suffocating, her lungs tight with each breath.

Snatching up her purse from the kitchen counter, she hurried from the house, aware of Lizzy's stunned expression as she'd flown through the kitchen. She hopped into the truck, intending to pick Sean up at the barn instead of waiting for him. Her hand trembled so badly, she had a hard time fitting the key into the ignition. When she accomplished that task, instead of starting the engine she just sat in the truck, staring out the windshield at the pasture where several mares grazed.

I'm as guilty as my father for putting conditions on my faith in the Lord, she thought. That realization struck her with the force of a hurricane, doubling her over. She rested her forehead against the steering wheel, thinking back to the times she had avoided going to church or praying because she had felt God wasn't listening to her. At the first sign of trouble she had turned away, just as her father had.

Dear Heavenly Father, please forgive me for all those years I thought I knew what was best. Help me to see Your way for me.

Sean swung the door open and climbed into the cab. "I'm all done. Let's go." He paused for a few seconds. "Mom, are you all right?"

Darcy lifted her head and focused on the most precious thing in her life. "I'm fine. I was just thinking, that's all." She would not cry. She would not fall apart in front of her son. With seesawing emotions, she asked,

"Are you all right with Grandpa not coming to hear you sing?"

He shrugged. "I guess so. Maybe he'll change his mind."

"Don't count on it, hon," she said, her hands clamping the steering wheel.

Finally Darcy started the truck and headed toward Crystal's house. After picking her up, they all made their way toward Sweetwater Community Church.

Crystal beamed. "Joshua came by and talked to Mom about a therapy dog for me. Isn't that great! I should be getting one soon."

"Then I can help you teach it some tricks," Sean said.

"Honey, I think therapy dogs are already trained," Darcy said, turning into the parking lot at the church.

"Yeah. Joshua said that if I drop a pencil, the dog can pick it up. That's so neat!"

"Way better than sitting or rolling over." Sean shifted on the seat. "I hope we're still here when you get your dog."

After parking along the sidewalk that led to the entrance, Darcy slid from the truck and came around to get Crystal out. Thankfully the child was small for her twelve years, so Darcy managed to lift her from the truck alone. But as she opened the door, Joshua walked up behind her.

"I'll get Crystal for you." He swung the wheelchair from the back and positioned it on the sidewalk.

Seeing him lifted Darcy's spirits. "Thanks. What are you doing here?"

"Myself and a few of the other firefighters at my station are the guest speakers today."

After Joshua placed Crystal in her wheelchair, Sean leaped from the truck. "I'll take her inside. Devotional starts in a few minutes. I don't want to be late."

Darcy stood next to Joshua, watching her son take care of Crystal. Her heart swelled with pride at how caring Sean was. Why couldn't her father see how important the talent show was to Sean?

"What's wrong, Darcy?"

She tilted her head to the side, looking into Joshua's beautiful blue eyes. "Nothing."

"Darcy, I'm getting pretty good at reading your moods and I've got the feeling something isn't right. Don't make me drag it out of you. I have to be ready to entertain the kids in twenty minutes."

He gave her a grin that sent her heart pounding. She said, "Dad and I had a big argument today. Sean asked him to come to the talent show on Friday evening and Dad said no. I couldn't—" Her emotions clogged her throat. She swallowed hard. "I finally told my father what I'd been carrying around for years." Tears misted her eyes, making Joshua's image blurry. "Do you know I can't remember my father ever telling me he loved me?" One tear escaped and rolled down her face.

Joshua brushed his thumb across her cheek, the touch so soft and gentle that her tears increased. Seeing them, he drew her against his rock-hard chest, his hand stroking the length of her back.

"I'm so sorry, Darcy. That can't be easy."

She cried against him, feeling the strong beat of his heart beneath her ear, soothing her, while his caress eased the disappointment she'd experienced all those years and was reliving now through Sean. For a brief moment she felt cherished by another, worthy of someone's attention.

Leaning back, she saw the wetness of her tears staining his shirt. She touched the damp place over his heart. "I didn't mean to cry like that."

"I know." He smoothed a stray strand of her hair behind her ear, then cupped her chin, compelling her to look him in the eye.

His soft expression threatened to bring on more tears. This man before her was special, someone who cared deeply for others, someone she actually might be able to love— She halted the train of her thoughts, not wanting to delve any more into her turbulent emotions, which had taken a beating that morning.

His intense gaze robbed her of thought. It held hers bound to him for a timeless moment. His other hand came up to fit along her jawline. Cradling her face, he leaned toward her.

Chapter Ten

Joshua brushed his lips across hers. Darcy's heart stopped beating for a split second, then began to hammer against her rib cage. As he settled his mouth over hers, she became lost in the sensations she hadn't ever experienced. As though Joshua realized where they were, he pulled back, his hands still cupping Darcy's face. Half veiled, his blue eyes smoldered. Reluctantly he slid his fingers away and stepped back.

Darcy sucked in a deep, calming breath, held it for a few seconds, then slowly released it between pursed lips. Joshua's kiss rocked her to her core as if he had laid claim to her. Every sensible part of her screamed that she should escape before she lost herself to him. There were so many reasons it would never work between them.

One corner of his mouth hitched in a lopsided grin. "I'd better get inside before they send out a search party. See you later."

Darcy didn't say anything, her mind swirling with all

the sensations that he'd provoked in her. The one over-riding thought was that she was in over her head.

"I'm so tickled to see you and Joshua together. My only regret is that I didn't get you two together," Jesse said, approaching from behind.

Darcy glanced over her shoulder at her friend and noticed the calculating gleam in her eyes. "You can stop right there. There is no 'Joshua and me.' Period. End of story, Jesse Bradshaw."

"Why don't you two come over to dinner next week?"

Darcy laughed. "No way. I know about your little dinner parties. I will not be a part of one of your match-making schemes."

Jesse shrugged. "What's there to match? It looked to me like you were doing pretty well on your own." She tilted her head. "Why *isn't* there a Joshua and Darcy?"

Fluttering her hand in the air, Darcy frowned. "Because—because—it wouldn't work."

"You're perfect for each other. You're much better for Joshua than Carol ever was."

"Did you get those two together?"

"They are not one of my failures, Darcy O'Brien. I'll have you know my record is quite good."

Darcy headed around her truck to the driver's side. "Well, don't get any ideas. Joshua is a friend who has taken an interest in Sean."

"Ah, a smart man. Going through your son to get past your defenses."

Darcy wrenched open the truck door. "What you see is what you get. I have no defenses." She climbed into the truck and started the engine.

Jesse opened the passenger door and poked her head into the cab. "You forget I was your best friend in high school and stood by you when your mother died. You have defenses to keep people from knowing the real you."

"Good day, Jesse."

Jesse closed the door, a knowing look on her face. As Darcy drove away, she tapped the steering wheel, nervous energy surging through her. She didn't have defenses. She didn't spill her life story to a stranger, but— who was she kidding? She knew perfectly well she was afraid to let anyone get too close, especially after her father's and Clay's rejections. She just couldn't deal with it a third time.

"Mom, do I look all right?" Sean asked, coming to a halt in front of her in the church's rec hall at the end of Vacation Bible School on Friday evening. He thrust back his shoulders and stood as tall as he could.

Darcy took in his black slacks and white short-sleeved shirt, his combed hair and clean face. "You will knock them dead."

"You think?"

"I know."

"See you after the show."

As Sean raced over to a group of boys standing near the stage, Joshua weaved his way through the crowd to-

ward her. Darcy also saw Jesse coming from the opposite direction. She'd better warn Joshua that Jesse was
up to her usual tricks. Darcy stepped forward to greet
him with a smile.

"Before Jesse arrives, I must warn you that—"

Joshua chuckled. "You don't have to. I've already
been subjected to twenty questions about us."

"She just doesn't understand there is no 'us.'"

"No, she's tenacious and honing in on us as we
speak." He grinned. "It's good to see you, Jesse. Is Nate
ready for the big talent show?"

"If Bingo will cooperate. He taught him to jump
through a hoop, which usually works until something
catches his eye and he runs off."

"Sean's trying to catch up with Nate on the dog
tricks, but Lady isn't cooperating. We'd better get a
seat. I want to sit up front."

Darcy led the way toward the front near the stage.
Joshua's nearness made her spine tingle, and she was
glad Jesse couldn't read minds. She would have a hard
time denying that Joshua was no more than a friend if
Jesse knew what she was thinking, feeling.

"Where's your dad, Darcy? I thought he would be
here tonight since Sean was performing." Jesse sat on
one side of Darcy while Joshua took the chair on the
other side.

"He had other plans."

Joshua slid his hand over hers and held it between
them. His reassuring touch chipped away at those defenses that Jesse declared she had.

The murmur of people's voices quieted. Darcy looked about, wondering why everyone had stopped talking—the show wasn't supposed to start for another ten minutes. Her gaze lit upon her father, with Lizzy next to him, striding toward her. An uncomfortable expression settled over his features. Stunned, Darcy scooted down so her father and Lizzy could sit by her.

The silence in the rec hall ended, and everyone seemed to be talking at once, greeting her father, waving at him. His uneasy expression evolved into a smile.

Her father slid into the chair next to Joshua, leaned over and said, "A guy can change his mind, too. That's not just for women."

"I'm glad you changed your mind. Sean will be thrilled to see you in the audience."

"He's the reason I'm here—him and you and Lizzy."

Her father threw the housekeeper an unreadable look that caused Darcy to wonder what had happened between them. She'd thought it strange that Lizzy said she would have to come later, that she still had something she needed to do. Lizzy had assured Sean, however, that she would be here in time to see him sing. Darcy studied the pair for a moment. She'd always thought Lizzy had a soft spot for her father, but Dad had seemed so immerse in his guilt and anger that Darcy hadn't believed her father had picked up on the signals from Lizzy.

Jesse leaned close and whispered into her ear, "It's about time those two got together."

Darcy chuckled. "They're not together—yet. And I agree. Dad needs someone to temper him and Lizzy would be perfect for the job."

"Maybe I should invite both you and Joshua and your dad and Lizzy to dinner."

Darcy's laughter filled the silence that had descended with the opening of the curtains on the stage. She blushed and whispered, "That would send my father running for the hills. You'd better leave well enough alone. Lizzy is more than capable of pursuing it from here."

"If you say so."

Joshua squeezed her hand, drawing her attention toward him. "I heard my name mentioned and a dinner party."

"Don't worry. I discouraged Jesse from going ahead with those plans."

He blew out a relieved breath and wiped some imaginary sweat from his brow. "Boy, that's a load off my mind."

Reverend Collins came out onto the stage and announced the first act: Nate Bradshaw and his dog, Bingo. Jesse clapped and whistled. The mutt lasted through two tricks before he took off, spotting something behind the curtain. Nate ran after him, and a laughing reverend stepped onto the stage.

The next act was Crystal and Sean. Her son wheeled the young girl out onto the stage and stood next to her. They sang "Amazing Grace," Darcy's favorite, and she was proud. The blending of Sean's and Crystal's voices was sweet and moving. Darcy glanced at her father during her son's performance and saw tears in his eyes. A lump formed in her throat, threatening her own tears.

When the pair were through, Darcy jumped to her feet and clapped. Her father, Joshua, and Lizzy joined her, followed by others in the audience.

The rest of the talent show sped by in a blur. Darcy was aware of Joshua next to her, aware of his every move as if they were connected. He no longer held her hand, but her skin tingled where he had touched her. Their comfortable camaraderie was shifting, evolving into something full of mystery and…hope. Startled by the direction her thoughts were going, Darcy pushed them away.

At the end she rose.

"Dad, thank you for coming. Did you see Sean's face light up when he saw you?"

"Yes. Did you hear him sing that song? I didn't know he was so talented."

"I think back home he should join the children's choir. I don't know where he got the ability to sing like an angel. It certainly wasn't from me."

"Your mother could sing like that."

At the mention of her mother, Darcy widened her eyes. Her father had rarely talked about her mother after her death. "That's right. I remember she used to be in the choir here."

"Yes, well—" her father shuffled around, glancing at the floor "—I guess it skipped a generation."

"Shamus, I need to make sure the refreshments are

set up correctly. Will you help me?" Lizzy asked, already heading toward the kitchen off the rec hall.

"See you later."

"Will wonders never cease? Not only is my father stepping into a kitchen, but he's going to *help* in one."

"Lizzy has a way about her." Joshua scanned the room. "I see Sean wheeling Crystal to Tanya. He's following your father into the kitchen now."

"I'm jealous. Us short people miss out on so much."

"I'm glad to see your dad here. Do you think he will start attending again?"

"This morning I would have said no. Tonight I have to say I don't know. My dad used to be predictable. Not now." Darcy remembered the tears in her father's eyes when Sean sang, and wondered about them. Had the words of the song spoken to her father on a spiritual level as they had to her?

"Maybe your conversation with him opened his eyes."

"Maybe," Darcy said, deciding she would have to pursue that with her father later.

Darcy entered the office at the back of the house and found her father standing at the large window that overlooked one of the pastures. Several mares grazed with their colts and fillies not far from them. The sun paved the green grass with its golden rays and the fields were dotted with multicolored wildflowers gently swaying in the breeze.

Looking out the window with her father, Darcy

couldn't help but think that the sight before her was God's work at its best. Beautiful. Serene. She'd forgotten how much she loved the farm—or rather, had forced herself to forget.

"Dad, we're just about ready to leave for the charity auction at the church. You still going with us?"

Never taking his eyes off the scene out the window, he answered, "I told Sean I would."

Relief trembled through Darcy. Her father had been acting strangely lately and she wasn't sure anymore what to expect from him. "Are you riding with Lizzy?"

"Yep. Joshua still coming by to pick you and Sean up?"

"Yep."

Silence descended between them, not the awkward kind of the past but a tranquil one. Again Darcy was surprised by that thought. In her mind tranquility and Shamrock Stables had never gone together before.

"Joshua's a good man. Sean really likes him." Her father shifted to look at her.

"Yes, he is, and your point being?"

He chuckled. "You're getting quite good at getting to the crux of what you want to say."

"I learned from the master."

"I'm glad you think I taught you something." Sadness darkened his eyes.

"I've always thought you taught me a lot. Everything I know about horses and farming is from you."

"But that's where it stops?"

"No, Dad. You were the one who taught me about the power of God."

"Until I stopped going to church." His hand lying on the windowpane fisted. "I was wrong, Darcy. I never should have, and do you know who made me realize that?"

Throat jammed with emotions, Darcy could only shake her head.

"Your son when he sang 'Amazing Grace.' I realized I was that wretched soul in the song. I've been going through life lost and blind. When Sean finished singing, I felt a peace over me that I hadn't felt in years—since before your mother's death."

"God works in amazing ways," Darcy said in a choked voice, her own reaction to the song swamping her with intense feelings. She, too, had turned away from the Lord in many ways—until she had come home.

Her father clasped her upper arms. "Exactly. I forgot that. I forgot the Lord is in control, not me, that He does care about us and is there for us. I have let my anger at your mother get in the way of our relationship as father and daughter. I love you, Darcy. Please don't ever think otherwise."

The roughened edge to her father's voice brought tears to her eyes. "Dad" was all she could say. Every other word was whisked from her mind.

He drew her into his embrace and gave her a fierce hug. "I haven't been the father I should have been. I was too tough on you because I wanted you to be ready to run this farm when I died. There was so much to teach you and you were all I had. I…" His voice faded into the quiet.

When Darcy pulled back to stare into his face, tears streamed down her face and she didn't care. For once she wanted to show what she was feeling in her heart.

"I was wrong, Darcy."

She'd never heard him admit that, and to hear him say it twice in one day stunned her.

"I won't make that mistake with Sean. I hope you'll let him come visit every summer. I hope you'll come, too. One day—" he motioned toward the window "—all this will be yours and Sean's. If you ever care to move back here, there will always be a home for you two."

"Dad, I don't know if—"

"Shh, you don't have to say anything. I understand why you stay away. Lizzy and I have been talking about it, and I can't blame you."

"Lizzy and you?" She shouldn't be surprised by that comment because she had seen them together quite a bit since his heart attack. Once the week before, Lizzy had been sitting at the dining room table eating her breakfast and conversing with her father. The second she had entered the room, though, the housekeeper had risen and scurried into the kitchen.

"I've come to depend on Lizzy as a friend." A glint entered his eyes. "Much like you and Joshua."

"Dad," Darcy said, warning him.

He held up his palm. "I won't say another word. We'd better get a move on or all the best items will have sold before we arrive."

"The auction isn't until the end. We eat first."

Her father started for the door. "I like that. A good plan. Fatten us up before taking our money."

"It's for a good cause. The outreach program at the church does some wonderful things."

"Yes, I know, Darcy. I'm the one who started it years ago."

"You did?" Darcy walked out of the office ahead of her father, realizing she didn't know him nearly as well as she'd thought.

"Yep. Reverend Collins and I came up with the idea over one of our Saturday morning coffees. I'm gonna hate to see him retire."

"He's retiring?" Darcy could only recall Reverend Collins as the pastor of their church. It would seem strange without him at the helm.

"He's been talking about it for the past few years. I think he will within the year."

"Mom! Grandpa!" Sean called. "Where are you? Joshua is here. We need to go." The shouts from the entry hall boomed through the house.

Darcy shook her head. "I think he wants to get going."

"With him I'm noticing it's all or nothing."

"You've about summed up my son."

"I'll go get Lizzy in the kitchen. We'll follow you all there."

"Mom!"

Darcy stepped into the foyer. "I'm right here."

"Good. Let's go." Sean raced for the door, threw it open and disappeared out onto the veranda.

Darcy faced Joshua. The small foyer grew even smaller with his presence. They were alone for the first time in a week, since the talent show. An eternity. She'd missed Joshua.

"Mom! Joshua! Let's go!"

One corner of his mouth hitched up. "Are you ready?"

She scooped up her large bag. "I am now."

On the drive to the church Sean chatted nonstop about the Fourth of July picnic, then the auction. Since the church wasn't far from Sweetwater Lake, he checked to make sure that Darcy had brought his swimming suit.

"Who's gonna be watching you all?" Darcy asked as they neared the church.

"Me for one. I volunteered to be the lifeguard from one to two."

"And have you had training?"

"Mom! Joshua can do anything."

Joshua laughed. "Listen to Sean. He's got it right. But to put your mind at rest, yes, I have had training. I was even a lifeguard for two summers as a teenager. I've also had paramedic training."

"See. I told you he could do anything."

Her son had a good case of hero worship, and the funny thing was, she did too. Joshua was the type of man she wished she'd met years ago before Clay. Then maybe she wouldn't be so cynical about love and marriage.

Joshua parked his truck near the picnic area because

he had brought his grill to use for the hamburgers and hot dogs. Lizzy, in the farm's truck with her father, had their contribution to the picnic—Lizzy's German potato salad.

Sean leaped down from the cab and raced toward his friends by the playground. Darcy, next to Joshua, her side pressed against his, watched her son until he was swallowed up in the crowd of children.

"You've done such a good job with him."

Sean had left the door open and a soft breeze cooled the warming air in the cab. Her heartbeat kicked up a notch and she found beads of sweat popping out on her forehead. "My, I may have to join the kids in the lake."

"Did you bring a bathing suit?"

"Yes."

"Then you can help me lifeguard."

"But I haven't had any training."

"That's okay. You can keep me company."

The intimacy in that last sentence caused perspiration to bead on her upper lip. She wiped away the moist film only to have it quickly reappear. Before too much longer she would be drenched in sweat and it would have nothing to do with the quickly climbing heat of July.

"Aren't you afraid I might distract you from your mission?"

He cocked his head, thought for a moment and said, "Now that you mention it, you'd better stay as far away from the lake while I'm on duty as possible. You in a bathing suit would be a definite distraction."

A rivulet of sweat rolled down her face. "Boy, I'm thirsty. I see Jesse is setting up the iced tea and lemonade." Before she was tempted to stay and find out what else was a distraction for Joshua, Darcy slid across the seat and exited through the open door.

She started to make a beeline for the refreshment table, then realized there were items in the back of the truck that needed to be unloaded. The twinkle in Joshua's eyes did nothing to cool her down. She needed to seek shelter from the sun—and Joshua Markham.

After taking the lawn chairs and a blanket to the area where everyone was gathering, Darcy strode toward Jesse. Darcy snatched up a paper cup and filled it with iced tea, then dumped several packets of sugar in the cold drink.

"So you and Joshua came together," Jesse said, taking a sip of her lemonade.

Darcy rolled her eyes and started to walk away.

"Avoiding me won't work, Darcy O'Brien."

She spun about, her hand on her waist. She took a step toward her friend and lowered her voice. "Just because you were happily married doesn't mean marriage is for everyone."

Jesse glanced over Darcy's shoulder. "One Joshua Markham coming in at twelve o'clock. Be seeing you."

Before Darcy could form a retort, Jesse had escaped and Joshua had reached the refreshment table. He poured himself some tea and downed it in several swallows.

"Where's Jesse off to?"

"Probably somewhere to cause trouble. I never knew

how troublesome she could be until—" Darcy clamped her lips together, realizing what she'd almost revealed to Joshua.

"Until you became the object of her matchmaking?"

"Right."

"Do you know she warned me against Carol years ago?"

"She did?" Darcy's estimation of Jesse's matchmaking skills was rising.

"Yes, said we weren't made for each other. And it turns out she was right."

"One out of how many?"

Joshua shrugged. "Who knows? She's always looking for love for everyone but herself."

"Odd, isn't it?"

"No, not really. When you've been hurt badly by love, some people would just prefer not to experience that feeling again, so they avoid it."

"But her marriage was a good one."

"Divorce or death can still produce the same kind of hurt. When you hurt because they're no longer around, it doesn't much matter how that came to be."

"Or when she leaves you at the altar?"

He checked his watch. "I'd better get moving. I'm in charge of grilling the hamburgers before my lifeguarding duty."

Darcy watched Joshua's retreating, ramrod-straight back. Why was she trying to force the issue with him? She was no more ready for a long-term relationship than he was.

While the men grilled the food, the women laid the side dishes out on the card tables under the large oak trees in the small field between the church and Sweetwater Lake. Darcy, assisting Lizzy, scanned the gathered crowd.

"Have you seen Tanya? She said she and Crystal would be coming." Darcy uncovered the salads and baked beans.

Lizzy's brow wrinkled in a deep frown. "She was supposed to bring her brownies everyone loves, but I don't see them on the dessert table."

"I wonder if something happened."

"You know Tanya. She's forgetful and—"

Her mind racing with all kinds of scenarios, Darcy dropped the spoon and hurried toward Joshua. Reaching his side, she grabbed his arm as he flipped over a hamburger. "Can I borrow the keys to your truck?"

He took one look at her face and asked, "What's wrong?"

"Tanya and Crystal aren't here. I'm worried. I—"

Joshua handed the turner to Reverend Collins and started toward his truck. "I'll drive."

"You don't have to go. I'm probably overreacting."

"I want to go. What if something has happened? Remember my paramedic training? Tanya can be fashionably late, but not this late."

Now Darcy *was* alarmed.

Chapter Eleven

Joshua made the short drive to Tanya's house in under ten minutes. The second he stopped, Darcy was out of the truck and running up to the door. She pressed the doorbell and kept ringing.

What seemed like hours later but was actually only minutes later, Crystal answered the door, tears streaking down her face.

Darcy clasped both her arms and squatted in front of her. "Oh, baby, what's wrong?"

"Mom. She won't get out of bed to take me to the picnic like she promised."

The hammering of Darcy's heart calmed slightly. "What did she say?"

The young girl sniffed. "Not much. Just that she was tired. But she's been sleeping for the past few days almost all the time."

Darcy straightened. "I'll go talk to her and see if I can get her to come with us."

Darcy found Tanya lying on her bed, the covers

tossed about as though the woman had been wrestling with them. Darcy went to the draperies and opened them to allow bright sunlight into the room. Tanya groaned and covered her head with a pillow.

Sitting on the edge of the bed next to Tanya, Darcy said, "You have a little girl in the next room crying because you aren't taking her to the picnic like you promised."

"I can't do anything right, Darcy. It's just easier to stay in here and not have to deal with things. It's not worth it anymore. It's just too much for me to deal with."

Darcy felt shaken to her core. It was worse than she had thought. Remembering her own mother and what had happened to her scared Darcy for Tanya. "I don't talk about this with many people, Tanya, but my mother was bipolar."

Tanya stirred, flinging the pillow away and looking at Darcy. "Your mother?"

"Yes. I know what Crystal's going through and it's frightening for a child. She thinks everything that is happening to you is her fault. But it's not. Something's wrong. Your medication is not working. You need to go back to the doctor, but you won't. My mother did the same thing. Finally her illness got the best of her, and I'm the one who found her when she killed herself. Is that what you want for your daughter?" She'd tried kindness. Now she was desperate and hoped tough love would prompt Tanya to get the assistance she needed to control her moods.

The woman blinked, tears rapidly filling her eyes. "No. I—I—" Her mouth moved but no words came out.

"You have a choice. You can stay here and feel sorry for yourself or you can get up, get dressed, and let me drive you to the hospital."

"Hospital?"

"I think you need to see a doctor right away, and since it's a holiday, that's the best place to go to get help immediately. Obviously things aren't working out right now. Your antidepressant isn't doing the trick. I'll help you if you'll help yourself. What do you say?" Darcy held her breath, afraid that Tanya would turn away and pull the covers over her head—like her mother had.

"What about Crystal?"

"Joshua can take her to the picnic and then to my house afterward. You don't need to worry about her. I'll take care of her. The important thing for you is to get help *now.*"

Emotions battled in Tanya's expression. Finally determination glinted in her eyes. She swiped away the tears and scooted to the side of the bed. "You'll help?"

"Yes."

Slightly dazed, Tanya combed her fingers through her stringy, dirty hair. "I don't know. I look awful. I need a shower. I haven't done laundry in days. I can't go anywhere looking like this."

"Get into the shower. I'm sure we can find something for you to wear. I'll have Joshua go on and take Crystal to the picnic." Darcy assisted Tanya to her feet. She wasn't giving Tanya a choice. She wasn't going to let her end up like her mother. She hadn't been able to help her mother, but she would Tanya. Then maybe the guilt she felt would go away.

Darcy strode to the living room and motioned to Joshua, who had been telling Crystal a joke. The child's laughter died on her lips when she saw Darcy. "Your mother will be fine. I'm going to take her to see the doctor."

Worry furrowed the young girl's brow. "Why?"

"Her medicine isn't working. The doctor can help her with that. She wants you to go to the picnic and have fun. Joshua will take you and then afterward you can come to the farm and play with Sean for a while. He could use some help with Lady."

Crystal started to say something, but didn't.

Darcy kneeled in front of the child's wheelchair. "Your mother will be all right, honey. Promise." *Because I won't let anything happen to her,* she added silently, her resolve strengthening.

"I do have a book I want to show Sean."

"Go get it. Then you and Joshua can leave."

Joshua waited until the child had wheeled herself out of the living room before asking, "Is everything all right?"

"I've convinced Tanya to go to the hospital. Hopefully she will get the help she needs. Her depression is getting worse. Something's wrong."

"Are you sure you don't want me to stay or meet you at the hospital?"

"We'll be okay. Crystal needs to go to the picnic. She needs to get out as much as possible, be around friends. I don't want her upset over her mother. Just take care of her for me."

"I can do that." He moved closer, lifted his hand and brushed his finger across her cheek. "I know your mother was bipolar. Are you okay?"

His touch sent comforting waves through her. She should have realized Joshua would be perceptive enough to pick up on her own sorrow surrounding her mother. "I won't sit by and watch Tanya destroy herself if I can do anything to help her. My mother committed suicide because she wouldn't get the help she needed. I'm gonna make sure Tanya gets help." She didn't normally talk about her mother and the way she died, but with Joshua it felt right.

"Aw, Darcy. I'm sorry. I didn't know." He took her face in his hands, stepping even closer.

His scent surrounded her in a soothing cocoon. His expression, full of support, nearly undid the composure that she was determined to maintain. Tanya needed a strong friend right now.

"I know this isn't the time nor the place, but I'm here for you if you need to talk."

The constriction in her throat prevented any words from forming. She leaned closer to him until only a breath separated them. Her lips tingled in anticipation of his kiss.

"I'm ready, Joshua," Crystal said from the doorway.

Darcy jumped away from him as though she had

been caught with her hand in the cookie jar. "See you two soon." Feeling a blush rise to her cheeks, she turned away and headed back toward Tanya's bedroom.

She could forget where she was when Joshua turned his charm on her. If this kept up, how was she going to be able to leave in five weeks with her heart intact?

Only two weeks until Darcy returned to Panama City. Easing down on the ground, Darcy couldn't believe how fast the summer had flown by. The dapple effect of the sunlight streaming through the trees mesmerized her. She propped herself against an oak, her legs stretched out in front, and watched the play of light on dark. Sounds—the flow of water over rocks, birds chirping, the rustle of leaves—punctuated the quiet. A crow's call pierced the air. One of the horses lifted her head and looked around, then resumed chewing on some blades of grass.

Her haven. Made even more special because Joshua was here beside her sharing it with her.

"*I'm* going to miss this," Darcy said, bringing one leg up so she could rest her arm on her knee.

"I'm going to miss it." Joshua eased down next to her. "I can't believe I don't get sore anymore when we ride."

"I'm sure Dad won't mind you coming out and going for a ride."

"It wouldn't be the same without my teacher."

She smiled. "You've been a good student."

"My teachers in high school would be surprised to hear you say that."

"You mean you weren't the model student?" She widened her eyes in mock shock.

"I know it's hard to believe, but I did visit the principal's office a few times. You know the old saying, boys will be boys."

"Don't let my son know that," Darcy said with a laugh. "I didn't get to ask you how the fishing trip went the other day. We didn't have any fish to eat that evening so I'm thinking it didn't go well."

Joshua's mouth curved downward. "Not according to my plans."

"Which were?"

"I had a big ol' catfish in mind for dinner. It just didn't oblige me."

"I don't understand why not." She shifted so she could face Joshua. "The important part was that Sean had a great time. He's now trying to talk his grandfather into going fishing. Dad won't have anything to do with it."

"I personally like to have a reason to do nothing. I'm always on the go, and to be able to sit back and wait for a fish to nibble is just fine by me."

"Why do you have to have a reason like going fishing to rest and take it easy? It's okay to do that every so often."

"This from a woman who is working twelve-hour days."

"That's so my father won't put in that kind of time."

His laughter echoed through the glade. "Darcy O'Brien, let's face it. You love working with the horses and running the farm."

No, I don't, she wanted to retort, but she knew that was a lie. She did love working on the farm, especially now that she and her father were getting along. He was continuing to teach her about the business, but this time he was also complimenting her when he liked what she was doing.

"In two weeks I'll have to put this all behind me and go back to my regular job. School starts the third week in August and I have to get the library up and ready to go."

"Which do you prefer, books or horses?"

His simple question stole the breath from her lungs. She averted her gaze, trying to figure out how to respond, surprised she didn't have a ready answer. A month ago she would have said books without a moment's hesitation. Now she couldn't honestly say.

"Why, I like to ride a horse and read at the same time."

"Nope. I'm not letting you off that easily."

"I've almost finished my part of the Sunday school lesson for this week. I love the story of Ruth."

Joshua laid his fingers over her mouth to stop her flow of words. "And don't try to change the subject. You're always prepared for the children on Sunday morning. It must be the teacher in you."

"Technically I'm not a teacher but a librarian."

"Do you deal with children every day?"

She nodded.

"Do you teach them about how to use the different resources of the library?"

"Yes."

"Then I think you're splitting hairs."

His fingers had fallen away but were now on her upper arm, massaging slow circles into her skin. She liked that he liked to touch her. Goose bumps pricked her from head to toe. She shivered.

"Cold? It's over ninety."

No way was she going to tell him that he could make her tremble with a mere touch. The smile that tugged at the corners of his mouth told her he knew exactly the effect he had on her. She was dangerously close to giving her whole heart to him. She had to keep focused on the fact she would be leaving in two weeks and wouldn't return until Christmas.

"You never told me which it would be—horses or books?"

"Haven't you ever had two options, each with its own special benefits, that you can't choose between?"

"I doubt when all aspects are examined that they would be equal. One would stand out over the other."

"Well, then my answer is that I haven't examined all aspects and can't give you an answer."

"You didn't think you would like managing the farm, did you?"

She shook her head. "Not when I showed up two months ago. I dreaded it. Now when I get up each morning, I look forward to the day." *Partly because you are so much a part of that day,* she added silently, wishing she could deny it, because she didn't see them having a future. She didn't think she could risk her heart again. The scars from her last encounter were still healing.

"I for one like seeing your father attending church again. It's a small church and we rely on its members participating in it fully."

"And have you seen Lizzy smiling lately? I definitely think something is going on with my father and her."

"It's about time."

"Why do you say that?"

"Everyone in town except your father knows that Lizzy has been in love with him for years."

"When it comes to relationships with people my father can be a bit slow. He's great with animals, though."

"Which I'm thankful for. I found a stray cat that he said he'll take. He wants one for the new barn going up."

"Helps keep the mice population down." Darcy tossed a pebble toward the stream and heard the splash as it hit the water. "Speaking of pets, Crystal is crazy about her therapy dog. I'm so glad you were able to help her get one so fast."

"I have a few connections. A therapy dog can help her to be as independent as possible."

"She's so excited. Can't wait to show the kids at church. She's actually looking forward to school starting in the fall. She thinks Charlie will be the hit of the school."

"He probably will be. How many kids get to take a pet to school every day?"

"I'm glad I don't have to testify at Tom's trial. Since he pleaded guilty, there won't be one. I wouldn't want to make things any worse for Crystal or Tanya."

"I think that's what made Tom not fight the charges. He'd put his family through enough already."

"They're still trying to pick up the pieces, but the church has been great to Tanya and Crystal. And Tanya even found a job yesterday."

Joshua's brows rose in surprise. "She did? Where?"

"At the bank as the receptionist. She's excited. She hasn't worked since before Crystal was born."

"When I've visited, she's been on more of an even keel."

"Yes, she's really trying to stay on her medication and promises me she will see the doctor regularly."

"She's lucky to have a friend like you."

"I just wish I could—" Her throat caught around the words she wanted to say.

"You could have helped your mother?"

She nodded, afraid to speak. Using her shoe to toy with a pebble nearby, she stared at the ground, not really seeing it. "I wish someone could have helped her. I was so young and really didn't even realize what was going on."

"But your father knew?"

Again she nodded.

"So for years you've blamed your father for what happened to your mother?"

"Yes," she said, her voice raspy. She clenched the pebble in the palm of her hand until its sharp edges cut into her skin.

"Sometimes people aren't ready to accept help, and no matter what a person does he can't change it."

"I know that now. Dad and I have talked. I know he tried to help Mom, but she just didn't or couldn't accept it. At least I know it in here—" Darcy pointed to her head "—I'm still working on knowing it in here—" She placed her hand over her heart.

"You weren't the only one affected by your mother's death. Your father was too."

"I'm discovering that. It helps to finally talk about it. For years my father wouldn't say a word about my mother, especially about how she died. There was a part of him that felt so betrayed. There was a part of me that did, too." She swung her gaze to Joshua's. "She's been gone for thirteen years, and yet almost every day that goes by, I still think about her. I never really got to say goodbye."

The rough pads of his thumbs grazed the skin under her eyes as he looked deeply into them. "A lot of people never get to say goodbye. We don't get to pick when we're going to die. People often leave behind unfinished business. That's why it's important to live your life to the fullest. Make each day count."

"I'm working on that." She laid her hands over his on her face.

Joshua bent forward and touched his mouth to hers. Her senses reeled from the sensation of his lips on hers, of his hands on her face, of his scent invading her nostrils. She was floating on clouds, soaring through the sky. Dangerous feelings bubbled to the surface—emotions of caring beyond friendship. A part of her wanted to surrender to those feelings, but years of hiding her innermost thoughts and emotions kept her from giving in to them completely.

She pulled back, his touch falling away. Something in his eyes told her that he was as surprised by the feelings generated between them as she was.

He shoved himself to his feet and extended his hand to her. "I'm on duty tonight. We'd better start back." A stiffness had entered his voice, his stance.

Darcy fitted her hand within his, and he tugged her to her feet. Releasing his grip, he walked toward his mare, untied the reins from a small tree and mounted. Darcy followed suit, her legs shaking from the emotions sweeping through her.

"Want to race back to the barn?" Joshua asked, guiding his horse from the grove of trees.

A meadow, tossed with wildflowers, stretched before Darcy. Off in the distance she saw the new barn being erected. A little to the left were three mares with their foals, grazing in the paddock.

"You do like to take risks. Are you sure?"

"I like to push my limits. I haven't ridden Patience at a full gallop yet."

"The last one to that gate over there—" Darcy gestured toward the one close to the new barn "—gets to cook a meal for the winner."

"What kind of bet is that? Neither one of us can cook."

"An interesting one." Darcy spurred her horse into a gallop.

Joshua shouted something behind her, and she glanced over her shoulder at him, laughing at his stunned expression. He prodded his horse into action. Wind whipped her hair behind her. Sunlight beat down upon her. She was one with her horse and happy, sharing something she loved with Joshua.

Her destination loomed ahead. The pounding of Joshua's horse sounded closer. Darcy was impressed. Joshua was a quick study. Slanting her head to the side, she caught sight of him out of the corner of her eye. Pushing her mare, she lengthened her lead, laughter rushing from the depths of her being at the pure joy of the contest.

She didn't slow until she made it to the gate. Reaching it first, she pulled up, twisted about in the saddle and saw Joshua only a few yards away. The expression on his face mirrored the elation she felt. Their gazes locked. Across the short expanse a connection formed and strengthened.

"I won!" Darcy said when he stopped next to her.

"You may change your mind after you eat the dinner I prepare for you."

The teasing glint in his eyes spurred her heart to beat as fast as her horse's hooves had pounded across the meadow. "Can't be any worse than what I would have fixed you."

"What a pair we make," he said with laughter, then leaned down to open the gate and allow her to go through first.

Yes, we do make quite a pair, she thought, directing

her mare toward the far barn. Next she would be thinking they were a couple. *A mistake,* her common sense
warned.

When Darcy reached the barn, she swung down
and began walking her mare to cool her off. Joshua fell
into step next to her. A comfortable silence was only
broken by the horses' hooves striking the dirt. She
sighed.

"I've had a nice time, Darcy."

"So have I." She headed into the barn to brush her
mare.

Inside, the cool shade offered a reprieve from the
summer heat. Her father and Sean stood staring into a
stall at the far end.

"What's up, you two?" Darcy asked them.

"Moonstruck is restless. She should have her foal
soon," Sean said, turning toward her. "Grandpa said I
can watch when the time comes."

Her father caught her eye. "Only if you give your
okay, Darcy."

Pleased that her father had sought her opinion, she
said, "It's about time he learns about that part of a breeding farm. Of course, Sean, most foals seem to be born at
night."

Sean squared his shoulders and drew himself up to
his full height. "I'll be okay. I can rest the next day."

Darcy secured the reins to a post, removed the saddle, then used a curry comb to brush the mare. With his
back to her, Joshua did the same.

As he watched Shamus and Sean leaving the barn,

Joshua paused and said, "Have you ever noticed that Sean does everything your father does?"

"Yes. This morning at breakfast he asked Lizzy for a cup so he could have coffee like his grandpa. Thankfully Dad persuaded him to wait a few more years before drinking coffee. I tell you, as a parent you always have to be one step ahead of your child."

Joshua peered over his shoulder at her. "Darcy, you are lucky to have a child."

Her teeth dug into her lower lip. She remembered Joshua once talking about how he had wanted children and had been devastated when Carol had left him at the altar, destroying that dream. At thirty-three he was cynical about marriage and leery of a deep emotional relationship. They definitely *were* a pair!

Chapter Twelve

"I don't smell anything burning. That's got to be a good sign," Darcy said, entering Joshua's house for the second time since she'd met him.

Joshua splayed his hand across his chest. "I'm crushed."

Ringo sauntered over to Darcy and wound himself around her legs, purring loudly. "What are we having for dinner?"

"A surprise."

"Do you even know yet?" She inhaled a deep breath. "Come to think of it, I don't smell anything cooking."

"Okay, if you must know, Trenton's Café is delivering—" he checked his watch "—in thirty minutes."

Darcy laughed. "I love Trenton's food. A man after my own heart."

"Then you don't mind?"

Darcy couldn't resist picking up Ringo and holding him close to her, rubbing her cheek into his soft fur. "If I had lost the bet, I would have pleaded for Lizzy to cook the dinner, and if she wouldn't have agreed, I would have done the exact same thing. So how can I mind?"

Joshua escorted her into the living room. "Good, because I have another confession to make. I tried to cook lasagna and failed miserably."

Darcy arched a brow. "Why didn't you try something easier?"

He sat on the couch, leaving her plenty of room to have a seat next to him. "Sean told me it was your favorite dish."

"You asked him? When? You've been gone these past few days." A rush of pleasure zipped through her. He had taken time away from his arson investigation in the eastern part of Kentucky to check with her son about her favorite food. Clay would never have done something like that. Her husband never even would have attempted to prepare her something to eat.

"I called him yesterday."

"That explains that silly smile he wore for half the day."

"I'm sorry about the lasagna, but thankfully Trenton's has it on their menu."

Chewing her lower lip, she glanced away from his penetrating eyes, busying herself by sitting down on the couch.

"Okay, what's up?"

Sighing, she smoothed her lime-green sundress. "Lasagna is my *son's* favorite dish, at least this week."

"You don't like it!"

"Oh, no. I like it. Really I do."

"What is your favorite food?"

"Fried shrimp. And yours?"

"A big, thick, juicy T-bone steak."

She relaxed back. "I'm glad we got that out of the way. I guess there's a lot we don't know about each other."

"We've only known each other two months."

"And I'm leaving at the end of next week." The reminder brought to mind all the reasons Darcy needed to keep herself from falling in love with Joshua. They really hadn't known each other long. She hadn't even known his favorite food, and he hadn't known hers.

Silence thickened the air. Joshua shifted on the couch, cloaking his expression and turning his attention to Ringo, who lay between them.

"In four months, I'm coming back for a week at Christmas." As she said it, the amount of time seemed inadequate. A week would pass in a flash. She would have her family obligations and Joshua would have his work.

"Sean said something about coming for the summer next year."

"I hope to. Even though Dad won't admit it, I think he would like the help." A nervous laugh escaped her. "I can't believe I'm saying that."

"You two have made amends. Now you can spend time strengthening those bonds."

But their relationship was still fragile, and with hundreds of miles between them those bonds might break.

Her breath caught. Who was she referring to—her father or Joshua?

"You didn't tell me how your trip was. Was the fire caused by an arsonist?" Darcy asked, needing to change the subject. This evening was supposed to be fun and light.

"Yes. Arnold discovered where the fire started. I gathered what evidence I could. I suspect it was set for insurance purposes."

"You've got Sean debating whether to be a breeder of horses or a firefighter. He's thinking he can do both."

"Sort of like you with your books and your horses? Have you ever decided which you prefer?"

"The jury is still out on that."

The doorbell chimed. Joshua rose to answer it while Darcy stroked Ringo, curled against her side. Which did she prefer? It really didn't make any difference. She was returning to Panama City in ten days. Her trip to Sweetwater, though, had shown her how much she missed riding horses. She would have to find someplace in Panama City where she could ride. Maybe one day she could even have her own horse again.

"Dinner has arrived," Joshua announced from the doorway.

He held several boxes, and the smells drifting to Darcy promised her a delicious meal. Her stomach responded to the aroma of tomatoes, meat and bread by rumbling.

"I'm hungry. I didn't realize how much until just now."

"It isn't fried shrimp, but Trenton's makes a wonderful lasagna with bread sticks and a Caesar salad. And for dessert a chocolate fudge cake that melts in your mouth."

Pushing herself to her feet, Darcy chuckled. "You could be a walking advertisement for them."

"I eat there several times a month. I'm a regular." He waved her toward the dining room.

She passed him and entered the room, coming to a halt a few feet inside the doorway. Before her the table was laid with china, crystal and silverware, all gleaming in the soft candlelight flanking the large bouquet of lilies, carnations and roses of red and white. "I'm impressed."

"I thought since I couldn't actually cook the meal with my own two hands that I could manage to set the table. These were my parents'." He indicated the dishes and utensils. "I haven't used them before now."

Touched by his gesture, Darcy swallowed several times to clear her throat before saying, "It's beautiful."

Joshua began opening the boxes to put the contents into the serving dishes. "I remember my mother pulling all this out for Christmas, Easter and Thanksgiving. She insisted on 'going fancy,' as she called it, those three times during the year. Every other meal was with our everyday dishes."

Darcy's meals with her parents hadn't made for happy memories. If her mother showed up, there usually was an argument between her and her father before the food grew cold, especially during the last few years before her death.

"We had a series of housekeepers. Usually they didn't last—until Lizzy came along. She's a trouper. She weathered my mother's ups and downs, and now my father's sullen disposition. She's a part of the family."

Joshua pulled the chair back for her to sit. Then he pushed the chair in and unfolded the napkin to lie across her lap.

"I feel like I'm in a fancy restaurant and not dressed properly. You should have warned me."

Joshua eased into the chair next to her. "And spoil my surprise? No way." His intense gaze held her. "You look great to me."

Dressed in a simple sundress with white sandals, she felt his attention riveted to her. From the expression in his eyes, she knew she was the only woman in the world. Long ago she had given up hope of ever being cherished by a man. But now Joshua was making her wish she wasn't leaving Sweetwater next week. He teased her with all the possibilities—if only they had more time to get to know each other, if only she wasn't so afraid, if only he wasn't still dealing with his emotions concerning Carol.

Seize the moment, Darcy O'Brien. She shoved her doubts and concerns to the back recesses of her mind. She would enjoy this evening and the man she was with. She would let him make her feel special for this one night, and she would cherish the memory.

"At least you didn't greet me at the door with a tux on. That would have sent me running back home to change."

He chuckled. "I don't own a tux. If I had my way, I wouldn't even own a suit. I feel like I'm suffocating when I wear a tie."

"That's the way my dad feels. Does any man like to wear a tie?"

Joshua shrugged, then passed her the crystal bowl with the salad in it. "Beats me. Not the ones I hang with."

After dishing up the greens, Darcy took the platter with the lasagna and spooned a large portion onto her dinner plate. "I can't believe this is still hot." Selecting a warm bread stick, she gave the bowl to Joshua.

"It helps that Trenton's is only five minutes away and that I'm such a good customer."

"And Sam Trenton goes to our church."

"Not to mention his daughter is in my Sunday school class."

Darcy filled her fork with some lasagna and slid it into her mouth. Ground beef, tomatoes, noodles and several different cheeses all mixed together deliciously. "Mmm. My compliments to the chef."

"I'll tell Sam the next time I see him." Joshua bit into a bread stick. "I did make the iced tea."

"Will wonders never cease?" Darcy tasted the raspberry-flavored tea. "Mmm. My compliments to the chef."

He inclined his head. "Thank you."

For the next few minutes Darcy ate, savoring the different favors and aromas. The soft candlelight and the elegant table setting lent an intimate atmosphere to the dinner. She became transfixed by the movement of Joshua's mouth as he chewed. Fantasies played across her mind, making heat rise to her cheeks. She looked down at her nearly empty plate.

"I guess this Sunday will be our last time to teach together at church."

She looked up at him. "You're right. I hadn't realized." *Hadn't wanted to think about it.*

"I'm gonna have to find someone to replace you. Any suggestions?"

No! The thought of someone replacing her bothered her. "Maybe Jesse." Even that suggestion made her frown. Jesse was single and would be great for Joshua. Darcy should be happy if they both were happy. But she wasn't.

"She would be good. I'll have to ask her this week. With my schedule I need a partner. There are Sundays I can't come because of work."

Partner. She'd always wanted to be an equal partner with someone. She'd hoped her marriage would be that way. It hadn't been, and now she didn't know if that would ever be possible. Someone always wanted to dominate— at least from her experience with Clay and her father.

But Joshua never has, a little voice inside her retorted. That was different. They weren't married—just teaching a class together—being friends. *Is it really that different?* the voice challenged.

Joshua scooted back his chair. "Wait here. I understand presentation is everything." He hurried into the kitchen with the last container from Trenton's.

Scanning the now empty dining room, Darcy realized she would miss Joshua more than she cared to admit. Sean would miss him, too. This was the reason she hadn't wanted to pursue a friendship with him—

Who was she kidding? Their relationship was beyond friendship and that was the problem.

"Ta-da!" Joshua produced two plates with pieces of the thick chocolate cake, caramel drizzled over them in a design. A few raspberries with a sprig of mint finished off the creation. He placed her dessert in front of her, then sat. "Well, what do you think?"

His eagerness made her smile as she sliced into the cake and sampled it. "I'll have to tell Sam the next time I see him how delicious this is."

"No, the presentation. I saw a cooking show and got the idea for this from it."

"And they say you can't learn anything from television." Her smile grew. "You did good." She took another bite, enjoying the rich chocolate mixed with caramel, one of her favorite combinations.

"When you're stuck in a motel room in a strange town, there isn't much else to do except watch what's on TV."

"I find it strange that you're watching a cooking show when you don't cook."

"I don't have to cook to appreciate the food being prepared."

When she finished off the last bit of her dessert, she said, "You've got the presentation part down pat."

"That and the tea are my personal touches. Do you want any coffee?"

"No. I don't drink as much coffee in the summer as I do in the winter."

"Then let's retire to the living room." He rose, putting his linen napkin on the table next to his plate.

"How about all this?" She motioned to the dishes left.

"You're my guest. I'll clean up later."

"Our bet said nothing about you having to clean up without some help."

"It's all part of the package, especially since you insisted on driving yourself to my house." He waved her toward the living room.

Darcy took a seat on the couch. "I have to pick up Sean at Nate's later."

"I could have done that."

"I know. But you've been away, and you have to work tomorrow."

When Joshua sat, he seemed to take up most of what was left of the couch. He was only inches from her and she felt the temperature rise.

"When do you have to get Sean?"

She glanced at her watch. "Soon," she said through dry lips. She ran her tongue over them and moistened her throat.

"When are we going to talk about us?"

"Us?" she squeaked, gulping.

"You know perfectly well what I'm talking about. We have something going on between us."

"What about Carol?"

"She's history."

"Is she, Joshua?"

"She's married. What do you think?"

"I think you still haven't dealt with her betrayal. You've avoided even thinking about her."

"Why should I think about her? She isn't part of my life anymore."

His defensive tone underscored Darcy's point. "When we went to Northland for lumber you were upset because Carol's husband was the manager. You have to deal with your past before you can really move on."

"Have you dealt with yours?"

"My father and I have come to terms."

"How about your feelings concerning your husband?"

Darcy stiffened.

"Just as I thought. You haven't dealt with Clay and the problems you two were having when he died."

"Why are you bringing this up now? Pushing me?"

Joshua surged to his feet and began pacing in front of the couch, rubbing his thumbs across the pads of his fingers. Then he stroked his jaw. "Because I don't want you to leave, but I realize I can't ask you to stay, either. Your job and your life is in Panama City." He came to a halt in front of her. "Yes, I *can* ask you to stay. I don't want you to leave yet. I care about you, Darcy."

Panic took hold of her. She craned her neck to look into his eyes, so full of uncertainty. She opened her mouth to reply, couldn't think of anything to say that made any sense, and snapped it closed.

"I want to see if we have a chance. Long-distance relationships are difficult at best. Won't you consider moving back to Sweetwater?"

There was a part of her that wanted to shout yes, but her defenses, put there by years of trying to be the perfect person for her father and husband, silenced her. "This is so sudden."

He kneeled and clasped her hands. "We've only begun to get to know each other. Don't leave next week."

"I need to pick up Sean. We can talk later. It's not something that I can rush into." So many emotions flew through her at the moment that she didn't know what she was feeling. She was confused, adrift. Joshua teased her with what might be, but neither one was really ready for the future. She couldn't afford that kind of risk. She had Sean to think about, not just herself.

He squeezed her hands, bringing them up to touch his chest where his heart lay beneath. "Come a little early to church on Sunday. We can talk then." He rose, releasing her.

Sunday was only a few days away. How was she supposed to make that kind of decision in such a short time? *Stay and we'll see if things work out.* Too risky.

She snatched up her purse and walked to the door. Her hand shook as she reached for the knob. Joshua gripped it at the same time she did and they touched. She pulled back, feeling burned, shocked by the electrical sensation streaking up her arm.

He had the ability to make her dream of more.

He had the ability to break her heart.

"Good night. The dinner was delicious." She escaped through the open doorway before she did something she would regret. She couldn't stay in Sweetwater, could she?

Perspiration drenched Darcy's face and neck, stinging her eyes. Quickly she lifted an arm to wipe her forehead with the sleeve of her shirt, then immediately returned her hand to help soothe the pain and panic reflected in Moonstruck's eyes, big and brown and dilated.

"You'll be all right, girl," Darcy whispered near the mare's ear. She wished she believed those words, but she felt dread. Moonstruck was one of her favorite horses at Shamrock Stables.

The mare tried to get up, but Darcy held her down while she looked back at the vet who was slowly pulling the foal from Moonstruck. Darcy brushed back damp strands of hair from her face, her gaze still trained on the vet while he attended the limp form of the foal, its glistening body barely moving.

Her worry intensified. She'd seen too much death in the past year. She felt as though a part of her was slipping away too. *This foal has to live! Please, dear Lord, breathe life into him.*

An hour later Darcy walked from the stall in the barn totally exhausted, glad that she hadn't gotten her son up for the birth as she had promised. Too many things had gone wrong from the beginning. She'd known Moon-struck would have a difficult time and she'd wanted to protect Sean from the sad reality that some foals die.

Outside she paused in the early morning and kneaded the side of her neck and shoulder, but her muscles had been coiled so tightly from the past few hours that massage did little to relieve her tension. The hot August air blasted her even though dawn had barely painted the sky with its pinks and oranges. The stifling humidity pressed in on her as she inhaled deeply, releasing the breath on a long sigh. The odors of hay, leather and horses laced the heated air, the familiar smells a reminder that her duty here would be ending when she left in a few days.

Arching her back, Darcy rolled her shoulders. She looked toward the main house but couldn't bring herself to take the first step toward it, to inform her father that they had lost a foal. Instead, she allowed her gaze to travel over the yard again, noting with satisfaction that the grooms were beginning their daily chores.

This was her home, her heritage. Could she move back to the farm and see where her relationship with Joshua would lead? He offered no promises, but he wanted to give them a chance. What did *she* want?

God give me a sign. Help me to decide what is best for everyone.

Fatigue urged her forward with leaden steps. She had to speak with her father before getting ready for church. He didn't like surprises, and she hadn't informed him that Moonstruck went into labor a little early. He'd been working so hard lately that she hadn't wanted him to miss his sleep, especially when she had discovered the foal was breech. As with Sean, she had wanted to protect her father for as long as she could.

Pushing open the back door, Darcy strode through the kitchen toward the dining room, briefly greeting Lizzy who was starting breakfast. The scent of coffee filled the air, prodding Darcy toward the pot set near her father at the long table.

"Where have you been?" Her father brought his cup to his mouth and drank.

Darcy poured herself some coffee and sank into the chair nearby. "At the barn." She sucked in a fortifying breath and continued. "Moonstruck delivered her foal early this morning."

Her father put down his cup, a storm beginning to brew in the depths of his eyes. "Why didn't you come get me? Everything okay?"

Darcy shook her head. "We lost the foal. The vet said Moonstruck is fine, though."

Shamus shot to his feet, nearly toppling his chair. "And you didn't think I should have been there?" Anger marked his features and his words.

Slowly, because her legs trembled, Darcy stood. "No, I thought you needed your sleep more. There was nothing you could do that the vet or I didn't do. Dad, you may have forgotten, but I haven't. You had a heart attack two months ago. I came home to help relieve the stress and workload for you so you could fully recover.

If you hadn't wanted me to manage the farm, then why did you agree to me coming back?"

Her father blinked as though her words had caught him by surprise. "Every birth is important."

"Yes, I know that, but you don't have to be at every one of them."

He drew himself up tall. "I always have been."

"You haven't really changed, have you?" Had she been fooling herself into believing she and her father could get along and run the farm together?

"You have. You never used to speak to me like this."

"Tell you what I'm feeling, what I think? No, I guess I didn't." Tired, disappointed, she grabbed for the cup to take it with her. "I'm going to get dressed. I have a Sunday school class to teach and a son to inform about the foal."

Darcy walked ahead of Sean, her father and Lizzy toward the church. She'd told Joshua she would come early so they could talk, but the last thing she felt like doing was having a serious discussion about her future, especially after her talk with Sean about Moonstruck and the foal. Her mind felt like mush and her body wasn't doing much better. Losing a foal on top of a night's sleep could do that to a person.

Maybe seeing Joshua's handsome face would cheer her up. She lengthened her strides toward the last classroom down the long hall.

"You will not believe the morning I've—" Darcy's words died on her lips as she entered the room.

Standing several feet apart were Joshua and Carol. She held a baby in her arms, patting him on his back, while Joshua scowled, his hands balled at his sides.

Darcy wished she could snatch her words back and silently exit the room before either one knew she had come in. No such luck. They both turned their attention toward her. The anguish she saw in Joshua's eyes made her own emotions swell inside her and threaten to choke off her next breath. In that moment she knew that she would never settle for anything less than having all of a man. She had settled all her life. She would not do that again. If Joshua wasn't over Carol, then how could they see where their relationship was heading?

"I'm sorry. I didn't mean to interrupt anything. I'll come back in fifteen minutes when the class begins." Darcy started to back out of the room.

"Don't leave. Carol's leaving. The nursery has been moved to the third room on the left."

"Thanks, Joshua. I appreciate the help." Carol glanced toward her. "You're Darcy O'Brien."

Darcy nodded, even though the woman hadn't asked a question.

"I was several years behind you in school. Are you home for good or taking a vacation?"

"Vacation. Leaving in a few days." Beneath the woman's polite tone, Darcy sensed a whole bunch of questions—the first being, what was her relationship to Joshua?

"It's nice to see you again."

When Carol disappeared through the doorway, the

silence pulsated with suppressed emotions, the air churning with feelings usually banked. Anger surged in her. *How could he make me fall in love with him when he still loves Carol?* Quickly that emotion slipped away to be replaced with relief. She'd discovered his true feelings before she had committed to staying.

"It isn't what you think."

"And what do I think?"

"I am over Carol." He pronounced each word slowly to emphasize the meaning.

"Are you? Maybe you didn't catch your expression in that mirror over there—" she flipped her hand toward the far wall "—but I was lucky enough to get the full effect from where I'm standing. *You are not over her.*"

Chapter Thirteen

"Carol came in here to tell me she was rejoining this church. She didn't want me to find out by surprise." Joshua eased his hands open and crossed his arms over his chest.

"How nice of her." Darcy felt the muscles in her face lock into a smile that she knew wasn't really a smile.

"My strange look was probably because she had just asked me if I wanted to hold her son. Her question threw me off guard."

"I think her whole visit threw you off guard."

He drew in a deep breath. "I won't deny that seeing her with her child bothered me. It did. We had planned to have a family. I want children."

And you should have children, she thought. Exhaustion still clung to her as though it were a part of her. Her only desire at the moment was to sit and do nothing. But stiffness spread throughout her body.

Uncrossing his arms, he started toward her, limping.

"What's wrong?" Darcy asked, fighting the urge to

back away. If he came near her, she would break down. She wanted to be a part of his life, but the encounter with Carol only emphasized the risks involved. Was she willing to take them?

"It's nothing." He waved away her concern. "There was a fire yesterday. Had some problems getting out of the house in time."

Nothing? She remembered her own close brush with a fire and knew the dangers personally. Fighting fires was a dangerous job, as her husband's had been.

Joshua clasped her upper arms, keeping a foot between them. "Listen, Darcy. Carol's in my past."

"So her and her family coming to this church each week won't bother you."

"I'm getting used to the idea. Remember, I've known she was planning to return for the past month. We won't be best friends, but I'm working on forgiving her."

"You haven't forgiven her?" His fingers burned into her skin.

"Honestly? No."

His admission underscored what she had known. It also confirmed that they couldn't have a future—at least not now. She wrenched herself free and put several feet between them.

"Seeing her son brought back all the plans and dreams I'd had. It's not always that easy to let go of that."

"Then how can you move on?"

"Stay and help me to. Take a risk, Darcy."

She shook her head, backing away some more. "I'm not one of your strays."

"I believe I know the difference between you and one of my strays."

"I can't stay. I can't do that to myself and Sean. I just can't."

Tears rose within, clogging her throat and misting her eyes. She wanted to flee, but at that very moment some of the children began to file into the room. She was trapped for the next forty-five minutes.

With his hands behind his back, Nate stopped in front of her. "Mrs. O'Brien, we sure are gonna miss you." He brought his arm around and presented her with a small bouquet of flowers, obviously picked from Jesse's garden.

Tears continued to gather in her eyes as each child gave her a token of their appreciation. Her son appeared last with a card signed by all the kids and a declaration that they were going to have a farewell party for her.

"You kept this a secret?" Darcy asked Sean as several parents brought in some lemonade and a chocolate cake.

"Yep." He puffed out his chest.

"This from the boy who makes me a present weeks before my birthday and gives it to me right away because he can't wait?"

Squaring his shoulders, he said, "This was different. I would have spoiled the surprise for everyone here if I had said something to you."

Her son was definitely growing up, and partially because of the influence of Joshua and her father. "Well, I'm impressed." She gave Sean a hug and a kiss on the cheek, which immediately caused him to screw up his face as though it wasn't something a boy of eight should get from his mother in front of a whole room full of his friends.

After a short devotional, Joshua stood before the circle of children and said to Darcy and Sean, "We wanted to show you how much we will miss both of you when you leave this week. The party is a small token of our appreciation for your filling in this summer."

"Speech. Speech," Nate called out from the back row.

Darcy moved to stand next to Joshua. "Nate Bradshaw, did your mother put you up to this?"

He nodded.

"I should have known. She knows how embarrassed I get when I have to say something in front of a crowd." *Just like Joshua,* Darcy thought with surprise.

"But you talked all summer when you taught us our lessons."

"Good point, Nate." Darcy cleared her throat, trying to keep her emotions in check. More than anything she wished she'd gotten a good night's sleep. Too many feelings were tangled up inside and so many were centered on the man next to her. All she had to do was move her arm a little and she could touch him—perhaps for the last time. Tears threatened to spill from her eyes.

"This means a lot to me." She gestured toward the table with her many gifts, mostly homemade and thus more endearing than store-bought ones. "I don't know what to say."

"How about telling us when you are coming back?" Brad Anderson asked.

"Yes, when?" Joshua asked, his gaze ensnaring hers.

"Christmas. Mom promised me we would come," Sean piped in, for which Darcy was thankful.

She didn't know if she could speak without her voice cracking. Through her misting eyes she took in all sixteen children, their faces turned toward her, their expressions, like their gifts, endearing.

"Why don't you stay?" Nate called out.

Darcy decided she needed to have a conversation with Jesse about her son asking questions he shouldn't. "My job is in Panama City," she offered, the reason suddenly sounding lame to her. A tear coursed down her cheek and she quickly brushed it away.

Why couldn't life be simpler? Why did emotions and the past have to interfere? Why couldn't Joshua love her with no strings attached? What was she afraid of? Questions bombarded her, making it difficult to keep control of her emotions. She turned away and swiped at her cheeks as the tears continued to roll down her face.

"We didn't mean to make you cry," Crystal said, wheeling herself into the room. "Sorry I'm late."

With one last brush across her cheek, Darcy spun toward Crystal, who stopped a few feet from her. She picked up a framed picture from her lap and handed it to Darcy.

She took it, her hand shaking. In the frame was a photo of her, Joshua, Sean and Crystal after they had completed the construction of the ramp. Everyone had big smiles as they showed off the product of their labor. She stared at Joshua in the picture with his tool belt around his waist and his arms about her and Sean. She and Joshua had laughed over the way the tool belt had slipped down low on her hips; if she had tried to move it would have slid completely off her. The photo would always remind her of a precious moment.

"Thank you, Crystal."

"No, thank you for the ramp and—" the child's voice faded while she dropped her head and whispered "—for my mom."

Darcy hugged Crystal. "You're welcome." When she stepped back from the girl, Darcy saw Tanya enter the room and wave to her. Who would be here for Tanya if she needed help? That question tugged at Darcy, making her decide to ask Lizzy to watch out for the woman.

The rest of the party went slowly. Darcy ate two pieces of cake and tried to laugh and smile, but inside she felt as though a part of her had died that morning. Her hopes? Her dreams? She wasn't sure, except that she felt empty. By the time the children had left to attend the service, all Darcy wanted to do was collapse into the nearest chair and lay her head down to rest. But first she needed to finish her conversation with Joshua.

After Sean had raced from the room with Nate, Darcy faced Joshua, who was throwing away the used paper plates. "We need to talk."

He jerked to his full height and swung around to

stab her with his gaze. "No, we don't. I think we said all we should say. Now, if you'll excuse me, I'm reading one of the lessons today in church and I need to go over the material before it starts." He walked toward the door, his strides long and purposeful.

Darcy watched him disappear out into the hallway. He wanted her to stay but couldn't offer her any guarantees. Yes, she had friends and family in Sweetwater. But what if she came home and Joshua couldn't move on in his life? How could she see him and not have her heart break each time? It was better to put this summer behind her and go back to Panama City. She knew what she wanted now—at least she had learned that much this summer.

Then why wasn't she happier about her decision?

On Wednesday, the quiet of the sanctuary soothed Joshua as he sat in the back pew, his hands folded in his lap. Was he going to let Carol continue to rule his life? He had wanted so desperately last Sunday morning to declare to Darcy that he'd completely forgiven Carol for walking out on him and marrying another. But he couldn't lie to Darcy no matter how much he wanted her to stay in Sweetwater. Lies were not what he would base a relationship on with a woman, especially someone as special as Darcy.

Lord, I need help. How do I begin to forgive someone who hurt me so badly? What is wrong with me? I've never had this problem before.

"Joshua?" Reverend Collins stood behind him, a worried expression on his face.

"I'll close up if you need to go home."

"That's all right. I normally don't bother anyone when they are in here, but something tells me you need to talk."

Joshua felt the weight of his inability to forgive press him down. His shoulders sagged. "Yes."

The reverend came and sat beside him in the pew. "What's bothering you? Darcy leaving?"

"That's part of it. I want her to stay, but I don't have the right to ask her to."

"Why not? I've seen how you two are together. I think you need each other."

"Because I'm still harboring ill feelings toward Carol. Darcy doesn't think I've moved on and she doesn't want to risk staying, with Carol still an issue in my life."

"Oh." The reverend was silent for a few moments, then asked, "Why haven't you forgiven Carol?"

That was a good question. Joshua wasn't sure he could answer it. Since she had left him at the altar, he had tried not to think about what could have been. He had pushed his emotions into the background, refusing even to examine them. Now Darcy was forcing him to take a good hard look at his feelings concerning Carol, concerning Darcy.

"Is it your male pride speaking?"

Joshua shrugged. "That could be some of it."

"You know the verse from Proverbs—pride goeth before destruction, and an haughty spirit before a fall."

"Yes, and I'm working on it. I think I would have

been all right if I hadn't been waiting for her in church in front of the whole congregation. I remembered their pitying glances for months afterwards. There had to be a better way to break the news to me."

"But that's not all?"

Plowing his fingers through his hair, Joshua frowned, staring at the back of the pew in front of him. "No. I've wanted a family for as long as I can remember. I was an only child and always said I would have a house full of children when I got married. Carol slept with another man, got pregnant by him when she was engaged to me. She had *his* child—not mine."

"What if Carol had married you, pregnant with another man's child? How would you have felt then?"

Joshua dropped his head. "Worse."

"Then Carol did the right thing by calling it off before you two got married. She only found out about the baby a few days before the wedding. She agonized over what to do."

"But she slept with Kyle."

"Yes, she made a terrible mistake and she had to face the consequences. After all, she's only human—just as we all are."

"And like Carol, I've made my share of mistakes?"

"Right. Think of all the mistakes God has forgiven you. Can you not forgive Carol this one mistake?" Reverend Collins rose. "I have some work to do in my office. Stay as long as you want."

"And be ye kind one to another, tenderhearted, forgiving one another, even as God for Christ's sake hath

forgiven you." The verse from Ephesians 4:32 popped into Joshua's mind. He knew what he must do.

Joshua marched up the steps to the front door and rang the bell. Taking a deep breath he squared his shoulders. A week ago he wouldn't even have considered doing this. Now it felt so right, he wondered why he had waited so long.

The door swung open. The woman framed in the entrance gasped.

"I know I'm probably the last person you expected to show up at your house, but may I come in?" Joshua asked, a calmness descending as if his past had been washed away.

"I just put Paul down for a nap." Carol stood to the side to allow Joshua inside. "What brings you by?"

Joshua walked into the living room where everything was in its place. Too sterile and neat for his taste, he thought as he turned to face the woman to whom he had once been engaged. "I needed to see you. I wasn't very inviting the other day at church, and I was wrong."

"I shouldn't have surprised you last Sunday."

"I knew you were thinking of returning to Sweetwater Community Church." He shook his head. "Until I did some soul searching, I was angry with you for the way you ended our engagement."

Her hands clasped in front of her, Carol averted her gaze. "I didn't handle that very well. I'm so sorry, Joshua. I had just found out I was pregnant and I knew you weren't the father. I seriously thought about going through with our wedding, but in the end I couldn't do that to you. That would have been worse than not showing up for our wedding."

"I'm the one who is sorry. I know you didn't ask me to, but I wanted to tell you I forgive you, Carol."

Her look flew back to his face. "Why are you telling me this now?"

"Because until I make amends with our situation, I can't really move on. I'm glad you're returning to the church. I know how much you enjoyed attending and I know you left because of me."

Her eyes clouded with tears; her hands twisted together. "I wasn't sure anyone would welcome me back, but last week no one said anything."

"They wouldn't, Carol. I'm learning that we're all human beings and we all make mistakes. So if God can forgive us, the least we can do is forgive each other."

She sniffed. "I appreciate you coming by."

Joshua started for the front door. Carol's words stopped him. "She's one lucky woman, Joshua. I wish you the best. You deserve it."

"Thanks." *I'll need all the luck in the world to convince Darcy to stay,* Joshua thought and headed for his truck. He wasn't finished with what he needed to do.

Darcy folded the last piece of clothing and put it into the suitcase, then closed it, the *click* of the lock sounding so final in the quiet of her childhood bedroom.

She hadn't heard from Joshua since Sunday, and she would be leaving tomorrow, early in the morning. With a glance out the window, she noted the gray tones of dusk settling over the land. Less than fourteen hours...

Her heart thumped against her chest in slow, anguish-filled beats. It had only been a few days since she'd last seen Joshua and she already missed him. How was she going to make it with hundreds of miles between them?

A knock at her door disturbed her thoughts. "Come in."

Lizzy entered the room. "I found this downstairs." She handed Darcy a black sweater she'd used when her father had cranked up the air-conditioning to freezing.

"Thanks. I'd forgotten about that."

"I can always mail you anything else you leave behind."

How about Joshua? Darcy instantly thought, a smile gracing her lips for a few seconds before disappearing.

"Or, you can get it when you come back at Christmas." Lizzy sat on the bed. "Frankly, I'd hoped you would be staying, Darcy."

"You did?" Darcy asked, wondering how she was going to manage seeing Joshua at Christmas. And yet, for Sean's sake and her father's she couldn't *not* come home.

"Yeah. I thought you and Joshua were getting along quite well. Your father might not say anything to you, but he doesn't want you to leave."

"He doesn't? He told you that?"

"You know your father and words. But I've been

with him for a long time and I've gotten to know him pretty well. He loves having you and Sean around."

Then why doesn't he ask me to stay? Darcy silently screamed, frustrated, even more torn up inside.

"Sean has enjoyed himself this summer."

Darcy held up her hand. "Hold it, Lizzy. No more. I know all the reasons I should stay."

"But?"

"But I can't. I just can't." Darcy turned away, busying herself rearranging her overnight bag to keep Lizzy from noticing how much her hands quivered.

"I don't see why not."

Darcy slid her eyes closed for a moment, then faced Lizzy. "Because I couldn't live in the same town as Joshua and not be with him."

"From what I've seen, you *are* with him."

Darcy sank onto the bed next to Lizzy. "He still has issues with Carol."

"Are you so sure that's the real reason you're leaving? Isn't it possible you still have issues with your husband and even your father?"

A heavy sigh whispered past Darcy's lips. "Yes, if I'm truthful with myself that's as much a reason as any."

Lizzy covered her hand on the bed. "I know your father can be a hard man, but he's trying to make things better between you. Darcy, it won't happen overnight, but if you stay away it may never get better."

"I'm coming back at Christmas," Darcy said defensively, knowing that really wasn't enough, not when she'd stayed away for ten years.

"Are you going to let your deceased husband continue to dictate how you're going to live? I've seen you change this summer and I think it's partially due to Joshua's influence. He allows a woman to be herself. He appreciates you for who you are."

"I know. But I was wrong about Clay. I thought I knew him, too."

"Some people are good at hiding behind facades. Joshua isn't one of those people. I've known him for years and he's always been very straightforward." Lizzy patted Darcy's hand. "But don't listen to me. Listen to your heart. What's it saying about Joshua?"

"I love him."

"Then why are you leaving?"

"Because I'm scared. I've been hurt before."

"So has Joshua, but he wants you to stay and see if it will work between you. Take the risk. Life is full of them. When you stop taking risks, you stop living life fully." Lizzy rose slowly, placing her hand at the small of her back. "This old body doesn't work like it used to. Think about what I said and pray for help. The Lord is wonderful to turn to when you have a dilemma."

When Lizzy closed the door behind her, Darcy stared at its dark wood, mulling over Lizzy's words. Darcy wanted to put down roots, had picked Panama City because that was the last place Clay had been stationed. But why couldn't she put down roots in her hometown? Sean needed his grandfather and, yes, Joshua if he would have her. She needed her father and most of all Joshua. Independence was great, but she would rather have interdependence—with Joshua, with her family. These past two months with Joshua had given her a glimpse of what a good relationship was like. He respected her opinions, even sought them, something Clay had never done.

Could she take the risk and stay?

"I am with you always, to the very end of the age." The verse from Matthew 28:20 was one of her favorites. She needed to remember that Jesus was with her through the bad and good times. With His strength and presence in her life, she could take the risk because she knew she would be all right in the end.

Darcy walked from her bedroom, intending to find her son, father and Lizzy to tell them she was going to stay. With each step she felt the rightness of her decision. Joshua was worth fighting for. What they had between them was good, and she was going to remind him of that. She would help him work through his issues with Carol instead of turning away from him as she had done. She had always run away from a problem in the past. Now it was her chance to stay and figure out a solution.

Downstairs she heard some laughter and headed toward the sound. In the kitchen she found her father with his arms about Lizzy, looking into the woman's eyes with an expression Darcy hadn't thought she would ever see again on her father's face. Love. Darcy's heart swelled at the sight of the two so wrapped up in each other that they hadn't heard her enter.

She coughed. They parted, looking surprised.

"I thought you were still packing," her father said, his cheeks flushed.

Lizzy began wiping down the already clean counter-top with quick movements, her head turned away.

"It's okay, you two. I'm glad you've finally come to your senses, Dad. Lizzy is a wonderful woman."

His flush deepened to a scarlet red. "Yes, I know. You don't mind?"

"Of course not. No one should be alone. And with that in mind, I've come to tell you that I'm staying in Sweetwater. If you'll have me, I would like to help with the farm for the time being. You need an assistant manager. You've been working way too hard."

Her father covered the expanse between them. "Are you sure, honey? I've never felt better in my whole life than I do now, but I would love the help."

"It's that diet that Lizzy has you on, and Lizzy's influence," Darcy said with a laugh. "*Yes,* I'm sure. I want Sean to know you. And I want to see where my relationship with Joshua goes."

"Ah, a good man."

"Mom! Mom!" Sean shouted from the entrance hall.

She started forward.

"Mom, Joshua's here to see you."

Darcy froze, her hand poised on the swinging door into the dining room. Her heart began to pound, her palms to sweat. She smoothed her hair back and glanced down at the shorts and oversized T-shirt she had on.

"You look great. Go get him," Lizzy said, standing again beside her father.

Darcy gave both of them a wink and pushed her way through the swinging door.

"Mom!"

"Sean, I'm right here. You don't have to shout the house down."

"Oh, I thought you were upstairs." Sean had positioned himself at the bottom step.

"And you couldn't go upstairs to get me?"

He grinned.

"I think Lizzy has some cookies for you."

Without another word, Sean raced toward the kitchen.

Darcy shifted her attention to Joshua, who stood by the front door as though positioned to leave if she wanted him to. "I'm glad you're here."

His brows rose. "I wasn't sure you'd want to see me."

"Until a while ago, I wasn't sure I wanted to see you either."

"What happened?" He took a step toward her.

Her heartbeat kicked up a notch. "I'm staying in Sweetwater. I just told Dad I want to be his assistant farm manager."

"Is that the only reason you're staying?" He came another step closer.

"No. Sean needs to stay in one place with people around him who care about him."

"True. Is that all?" Joshua moved two more steps until he was in front of her, an arm's length away.

"But mostly, I'm staying because of you."

"Why?"

"Because I love you and I want to see if there is an 'us.'"

He drew her against him. "I can tell you there definitely is an us." His lips settled over hers in a long kiss.

When he pulled back to look into her eyes, Darcy smiled, still feeling the tingling sensation his kiss had produced throughout her body. "What's changed? There's something about you that is different."

"I took your advice and dealt with my past. I went to see Carol before I came here. I told her I forgave her for leaving me at the altar." He snuggled closer. "And I meant every word I said. I want her to be happy because I'm happy. I love you, Darcy O'Brien."

"Are you sure?"

"Yes. Are you?"

"Yes. I want to stay and see where this relationship leads us." She laid her head against his chest, listening to the hammering of his heart that matched the fast tempo of hers. "We have all the time in the world to get to know each other. I'm not going anywhere, Joshua Markham."

Epilogue

Dressed in a black tuxedo, Joshua straightened to his full height, rubbing his thumbs across the tips of his fingers. Scanning the crowd in the sanctuary, he saw the expectant faces of his friends and family. Next to him stood Sean in a similar tux, a huge grin on his face.

The people in the church fell silent. The organ stopped for a few seconds, then started again. Joshua held his breath, his lungs burning. Tanya appeared in a pink satin dress pushing Crystal's wheelchair. Crystal wore the same type of dress as her mother and her dark hair was pulled on top of her head in curls with glittering stars peeking out. The young girl tossed pink rose petals down the long aisle as her mother rolled her toward the altar.

Only a moment longer, Joshua told himself, beginning to feel the constriction about his neck from his tie. Sean gave Crystal a thumbs-up when she went by him to sit next to the front pew on the left-hand side.

Then Jesse appeared at the back in a different version of the pink satin that Crystal wore. As she neared

Joshua, she winked at him, then went to stand on the other side.

Suddenly the organ music changed to "The Wedding March." Everyone rose and turned to the back. Joshua forced himself to release his pent-up breath, his gaze riveted to the empty place where Darcy should be.

One second… Two… Then he saw her and pure joy swept through him. Never in his life had he seen such a beautiful sight as his soon-to-be wife walking down the aisle on her father's arm toward him, dressed in a long, cream-colored gown of lace and satin. Her smile filled his vision, his heart. He would soon have the family he'd always desired.

Darcy slipped her hand in Joshua's with all the self-assurance that she was making the best decision of her life. *What a perfect day to get married,* she thought. *Valentine's Day. A day for lovers. A day for beginnings.*

Her father kissed her on the cheek. "You take good care of her, son."

"I will, sir."

And Darcy knew Joshua would. Together they turned to face Reverend Collins as equal partners, with Darcy eager to start her new life.

* * * * *

The matchmaker meets her match when
Darcy's friend Jesse Bradshaw finds love in
A MOTHER FOR CINDY
coming in January 2005,
only from Margaret Daley and Steeple Hill!

Dear Reader,

In my first book in THE LADIES OF SWEETWATER LAKE series, *Gold in the Fire*, I explore the topic of people taking emotional risks in their lives. It is important to learn to put our trust in God and not to shy away from change. Life is full of changes that we need to embrace, but those changes can be scary. With faith in the Lord we can be better prepared to accept the changes and risks. Darcy had to learn this with the help of Joshua. For Darcy, coming back home was full of emotional risks—first with her father, then with Joshua. But Darcy wasn't the only one in the story who had to take an emotional risk; Joshua put his life on the line many times working as a firefighter. In his personal life he didn't take any risks at all—until Darcy forced him to through her love.

In THE LADIES OF SWEETWATER LAKE, five women form a bond of friendship to help each other through tough times. Darcy's story is the first one in the series. In January 2005, the second book, *A Mother for Cindy*, will be published. This features Jesse Bradshaw, the town matchmaker and Darcy's good friend. Then in April 2005 comes the third story, *Light in the Storm*, about Beth Coleman, another member of the circle of friends.

I love hearing from readers, You can contact me at P.O. Box 2074, Tulsa, OK, 74101 or visit my Web site at www.margaretdaley.com.

Best wishes,

Margaret Daley

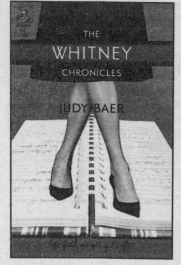